SUSAN TRACY
Yesterday's Bride

Silhouette Romance

Published by Silhouette Books New York

America's Publisher of Contemporary Romance

SILHOUETTE BOOKS, a Simon & Schuster Division of
GULF & WESTERN CORPORATION
1230 Avenue of the Americas, New York, N.Y. 10020

ISBN: 0-671-57159-1

First Silhouette Books printing June, 1982

10 9 8 7 6 5 4 3 2 1

"Why Did You Run Away?" Jason Asked.

"Because I found out why you married me!"

"And why was that?"

"You needed a wife and I happened to be available."

The dark eyes narrowed. His face was a cold, hard mask.

"You should have made it clearer to me! I was young. I stupidly assumed that you loved me. . . ."

"Love!" He spat out the word. "You can't base a marriage on illusion."

Leigh flinched with pain.

"Our marriage could have worked, Leigh," he added more softly. "You should have given it a chance."

SUSAN TRACY
is another of our American authors. She has lived most of her life below the Mason-Dixon line, and likes to set her novels in the region that she knows and loves. An enthusiastic amateur photographer, her interest in capturing personality is reflected in her thoughtful treatment of her fictional characters.

Dear Reader:

During the last year, many of you have written to Silhouette telling us what you like best about Silhouette Romances and, more recently, about Silhouette Special Editions. You've also told us what else you'd like to read from Silhouette. With your comments and suggestions in mind, we've developed SILHOUETTE DESIRE.

SILHOUETTE DESIREs will be on sale this June, and each month we'll bring you four new DESIREs written by some of your favorite authors—Stephanie James, Diana Palmer, Rita Clay, Suzanne Simms and many more.

SILHOUETTE DESIREs may not be for everyone, but they are for those readers who want a more sensual, provocative romance. The heroines are slightly older—women who are actively involved in their careers and the world around them. If you want to experience all the excitement, passion and joy of falling in love, then SILHOUETTE DESIRE is for you.

I'd appreciate any thoughts you'd like to share with us on new SILHOUETTE DESIRE, and I invite you to write to us at the address below:

Karen Solem
Editor-in-Chief
Silhouette Books
P.O. Box 769
New York, N.Y. 10019

To Susan and Jill

Yesterday's Bride

Chapter One

"Amen." The minister ended the prayer and lifted his head. The service was over. As they moved away, several of the mourners stopped to speak to the girl standing beside the open grave, a forlorn figure with her bowed head and hunched shoulders.

Rain that had threatened all day began to fall in a fine mist from leaden skies. A chill wind, more characteristic of March than April, had sprung up and was moving the branches of the few trees shading the cemetery. It was a grim scene, but the girl seemed not to notice. She was staring at the ground, her face giving no clue to her thoughts.

Leigh Melville had just buried her grandfather, the Judge. She would miss him terribly. He had brought her up, and even if they hadn't seen much of one another in the last few years, they had still been close. She could always count on him to understand, whatever the circumstances. And she had certainly presented him with some difficult circumstances, thought Leigh wryly. Well, she squared her slender shoulders and took a deep breath, he was gone, and although she would never forget him or what he had done for her, she would put the past behind her.

Leigh started as someone touched her arm. A plump, middle-aged woman wearing a black coat said gently, "It's time to go, Miss Leigh. Come on, you'll get drenched." She urged the girl forward. "There's nothing more we can do here." Flora Martin, the Judge's housekeeper, propelled Leigh toward the cemetery gate.

As she walked down the graveled path between the headstones, Leigh noticed a tall man standing alone by the gate. Although his face was in shadow, he was looking directly at Leigh and she recognized him immediately.

She stopped and grabbed at Flora's hand, not taking her eyes off the figure ahead. "I should have known he'd be here," she murmured to herself. "He always admired and respected Grandfather."

Turning to Flora she asked, "Would you wait for me in the car? I'll only be a minute."

The older woman glanced apprehensively at the man standing a few feet away. "Are you sure, Miss Leigh? Why don't you just come on with me now? You've been through enough for one day," she prompted loyally.

10

"I'm all right, Flora," the girl answered. "Go on to the car."

Leigh was more shaken than she would have admitted and she wanted to get the next few moments over with as quickly as possible. She schooled her features into a cool mask, thanking her stars she had been so well trained.

Walking toward him Leigh got a clearer view of his face. He looks older, she decided. Harsh lines that hadn't been there five years ago etched his mouth and eyes and flecks of gray glinted in the thick black hair. But he was still lean, rugged, too attractive for comfort with that controlled strength of his, that air of being capable of handling anything or anyone.

Leigh had thought, if she ever saw him again, that she would find his magnetism diminished. After all, she had been so young when she knew him. But it wasn't her youthful inexperience that had imbued him with his power. Anywhere in the world, in any company, she knew this man would stand out.

His brown eyes stared without expression into her gray ones—she never had known what he was thinking—as he stood there silently, waiting for her to speak.

"Hello, Jason."

He inclined his head to acknowledge her greeting. "I'm sorry about your grandfather, Leigh. He was a fine man."

She tried to relax. "Yes, he was. Thank you for coming, Jason."

Again he nodded, his eyes never leaving her face.

Leigh took a breath. "Jason," she said, "I'd like to talk to you."

The level black brows raised. "Of course," he assented, "go ahead."

Leigh moistened her dry lips and forced the words from a constricted throat, "Not now, Jason, and not here. Could we make an appointment, some time that would be convenient for you?"

"Such consideration," he said softly. "I take it you won't be rushing right away."

Leigh hated him so much she was shaking, and it took all her control to answer calmly, "No, there are legal matters to clear up. I'll probably be in Raleigh for a few more days."

She couldn't look at him anymore so she peered over his shoulder at the rain-washed street.

Jason paused briefly before asking, "How does tomorrow suit you—around five? Are you staying at the house?"

"Tomorrow's fine. Yes, I'm at the house." Leigh gripped her hands tightly together. "I'll see you then."

Without waiting for an answer she walked quickly past him, through the gateway, and stumbled hurriedly into the back of the waiting limousine. As she sank into the cushions, Leigh closed her eyes. *I have to pull myself together,* she thought. *He's not worth getting upset over. It's just the shock of seeing him so suddenly, without warning.*

With a worried expression on her face, Flora watched Leigh. Rarely had she seen the girl look so vulnerable. Usually she was cool and serene with a slightly detached air about her. *And so lovely*, thought the woman. Hair that looked more silver than blond, a small, straight nose, a sweet mouth. Although rather tall and quite capable, Leigh sometimes gave the impression of fragility, perhaps because she was slender or perhaps because of the fey expression that could come into her wide gray eyes.

Turning to Flora, Leigh grasped at her composure and forced herself to speak evenly. "I haven't had a chance to talk to you properly since I arrived yesterday," she said. "The house has been so full of people. The Judge was well thought of, wasn't he?"

The housekeeper wiped at her reddened eyes. "Oh, Miss Leigh, what are we going to do without him? He was such a good, kind man." She began to weep again.

After a while Leigh took the woman's workworn hand in hers and asked about her plans.

"I thought I'd go to my sister in Wilmington. She's a widow, living alone, and would welcome some company. I hate leaving Raleigh though, it's been my home for such a long time."

"I wish you would come back to New York with me. I'd love having you to spoil me again. Remember how you used to make me those delicious ginger cookies and then scold me for eating too many?"

Flora scowled and shook an admonishing finger in Leigh's face. "You look as if you need some good nourishing food. I've never seen you so thin. You'll blow away one fine day."

Leigh smiled at her. "I'm a model. The camera adds inches, you know. If I gain too much weight, I won't photograph well and then what would I do?"

Flora sniffed and said gruffly, "You could stay here."

Sadly Leigh shook her head. "My life is in New York now, more so than ever with Grandfather gone." She looked out the window as the car slowed. "We're home."

The limousine, provided by the funeral service, pulled up in front of an imposing white Victorian house, and Leigh leaned across the front seat to thank the driver and the representative from the funeral home who had ridden with them. Then she slid out of the car, took Flora's arm and hurried into the house.

As they stood in the hall shaking the rain from their coats, Leigh swallowed a lump in her throat. This house won't be home much longer, she thought. Suddenly the events of the past two days caught up with her. The phone call from Flora that the Judge had had a fatal heart attack. Rushing to get here. Trying to stay calm to talk to the dozens of people who had called, bringing sympathy and food in the Southern tradition—neighbors, old friends of the Judge, people he had helped. Finally, the strain of the funeral. Now the house was quiet. Their friends were considerately giving Flora and Leigh solitude in which to deal with their grief.

"I'll make some tea," Flora offered, looking into Leigh's drawn face.

"No, thank you, Flora," Leigh answered with difficulty. "I think I'll just go to my room. I'd like to be alone for a while." And with that, Leigh fled up the stairs to find what solace she could.

The next morning, both wan-faced and red-eyed, Leigh and Flora were up early, armed with a long list of things to do. Leigh dressed practically in faded denim jeans and an old blue shirt. Before starting, she allowed herself only a cup of Flora's aromatic coffee and one of the ham biscuits that a neighbor had thoughtfully provided.

The first thing she did was to call a real estate agent and place the house on the market. Then, while Flora was packing up kitchen items, Leigh attacked the Judge's study. She had set herself a difficult task for she sensed her grandfather's presence so strongly here, the scent of his tobacco pervading the room. It was to the study that the child Leigh had brought her school reports, had been summoned after mischief, and later, had come to have long, serious talks with her grandfather when she needed advice or guidance.

The study was large, its walls book-lined except for where French windows opened into the garden. Leigh could remember her grandfather strolling to look out those windows when he was deep in thought or when something was troubling him. She walked over to the massive roll-top desk that dominated the room and began the painful task of going through its contents.

By lunchtime Leigh and Flora had finished with all the downstairs rooms, packing away whatever was not to be sold with the house. Leigh wondered how some prospective buyer would feel about the furniture—the ornate, stiff couch with its plush cover, the whatnot shelves, the dark mahogany dining table and sturdy carved chairs, the china cabinet whose treasures Leigh had loved to plunder when she was a child. Leigh's grandmother had decorated the house when sturdiness and formality were the arbiters of taste, and the Judge had never changed a thing, other than the necessary modernizations.

As they sat down in the kitchen to chicken sandwiches and coffee, Leigh and Flora made plans for the afternoon.

"I don't know about you, but I could do with a rest," said Leigh, biting into her sandwich. "All that bending! Every muscle in my body aches and I'm so grimy that I'll probably leave smudges everywhere I go."

"A rest sounds good to me," answered Flora, putting another sandwich on Leigh's plate. "Then we can tackle the rooms upstairs." She hesitated, concern in her kindly blue eyes. "You'll have to go through your old bedroom, Miss Leigh. I'd clear it for you if I could, but there are things in there that only you know what to do with." Flora paused again before continuing. "You know that no one has used that room since you left home."

"It's OK, Flora," Leigh reassured her. "It was silly of me not to sleep there on my visits home, but I just never could. Nothing's in that room but dusty old memories. I'll pack it up if you'll do the guest rooms and the Judge's room. We can decide later about his personal things."

Leigh pushed back from the table and stretched out her legs. "I'm going to collapse on the front porch for an hour," she said.

"Not until you sample this pecan pie," Flora stated with a determined look in her eye.

After they had cleared the table and washed the few dishes, the housekeeper went to her room off the kitchen to nap and Leigh headed for the porch. She sat down on the swing that was suspended by chains from the ceiling, rested her head, and idly pushed back and forth. Leigh had always loved sitting on the porch with the Judge on warm summer evenings after supper. They would listen to the crickets or Leigh would race around the yard to catch fireflies and put them in jars with holes punched in the lids. And later she and Jason used to sit in the swing when he brought her home from their dates. Even when the weather was cold, they would cuddle up and talk. Better not dwell on that, thought Leigh, jumping to her feet.

"I'm going upstairs to exorcise some ghosts," she announced as she marched inside, letting the door swing to behind her with a bang.

She ran up the stairs and threw open the door to her old room. It's just the same, she reflected as she looked around. The bedroom was pretty and very feminine, with white and gold French provincial furniture that suited Leigh somehow. Covered with a white organdy spread and topped by a lacy canopy, the bed was the focal point of the room. Leigh slowly trailed her hand across its pristine coverlet, a faraway look in her eyes.

It was the room of a young girl. The Judge had had it decorated for her as soon as she had come to live here, after the automobile accident that took her parents' lives. She had been eight years old, bewildered and frightened, but the Judge's kindness and Flora's brusque mothering had soon made her feel at home. She had had a good childhood in this house, perhaps a rather solitary one spent more with adults than other children, but a happy time nonetheless.

Wandering to the row of windows set in the wall opposite the door, Leigh leaned her head against a windowpane and stared unseeingly out. Some of her memories were painful, but she knew she must take them out, examine them and thrust them behind her forever.

Leigh closed her eyes, thinking back five years. She had been thrilled, she remembered, and more than a little apprehensive when the Judge had told her that he wanted her to make a debut into Raleigh society. The debut would be good for her, he explained, it would make her more at ease socially, polish her off. At eighteen, in her first year at St. Mary's Junior College, she was overly sensitive and young for her years and a bit shy with boys and girls her own age, but somehow she had gotten through the ordeals of teas, parties and dances, and had even relaxed enough to enjoy them. She never lacked for partners and soon learned to engage in the nonsensical chatter that was expected of her.

Then came the highlight of her presentation to society, the Governor's Ball. Dressed in flowing white chiffon, her silver hair caught high on her head, she was quite the most striking girl there.

Trying to catch her breath from the whirl of dancing, Leigh was resting on the sidelines when one of the sponsors of the Ball approached her. Clare Randall, a petite brunette, was a former debutante who was helping to organize this season's festivities. "I have someone here who wants to be introduced to you," she told Leigh. "May I present my brother-in-law, Jason Randall. Jason, Miss Melville."

Leigh looked up expecting to see another college boy, as most of the escorts at the Ball were, but no callow youth stood before her. He must be approaching thirty, she surmised, studying the man through her lashes.

Jason Randall was not handsome, his features were too uncompromising for that. But his was a face full of character. Not an easy man to know, Leigh felt, unless he wanted you to know him, but nonetheless a man you could depend on. She could feel his strength and competence. And he's tough, Leigh decided as she summed him up mentally.

He was a man wholly outside Leigh's range of experience, used as she was to people her own age or considerably older. With a nervous smile, she gave him her hand and said a prim how do you do.

When he smiled, he took her breath away. The smile softened his strong features, making him look younger, even more vital, if that was possible. Watch out, Leigh warned herself, this one's a lady-killer.

His voice was low and attractive, with a slight drawl. "Will you dance with me?" he asked, and almost mesmerized, Leigh gave him her hand and let him lead her onto the dance floor.

"Miss Leigh Melville," he said as if savoring her name. "I wanted to meet you very badly."

Leigh didn't know what to say.

After they had circled the floor a few times in silence, Jason looked down into her gray eyes and asked, "Do you have a steady boyfriend?"

"No, but . . ." Leigh didn't know how to handle this. He was moving too swiftly for her.

Jason cut into her reply. "Good! We're going to get to know each other better, you and I, and a boyfriend would have been in the way."

Leigh gasped. "You don't waste any time, do you?"

Brown eyes raked her face. "Not if it's something I want," he answered slowly.

Her cheeks burning with anger, Leigh spat out, "You are the most insufferable, arrogant, conceited creature it has ever been my misfortune to meet. In the first place, if I had a dozen boyfriends, it's none of your business. You're a stranger and likely to stay that way. And secondly, what makes you think I would go out with you even if the alternative were to sit home alone every night of my life?"

Breathless from the spate of words, Leigh began to struggle out of his arms.

"Hey, hold on, you don't want to cause a scene. I'll behave." He loosened his hold on her. "I've never been any good at small talk. If I have something to say, I just say it. Maybe I was precipitous and not very adept, but all I was trying to do was tell you that I'd like to see you again," he apologized with a sheepish grin. The grin was not quite as devastating as the smile, but Leigh felt her anger sliding away.

"I'm just a country boy, after all. I don't know how to behave with society ladies," he teased, the grin broader than ever.

Leigh wasn't sure she shouldn't end this conversation and this dance right now. "I get the feeling you're making fun of me," she said.

"Never," he intoned solemnly. "I do apologize and beg you to let us start over. I'll even get down on my knees."

Leigh's indignation turned to laughter, as he had intended it to. "I doubt if you often apologize or beg, so how can I refuse you?" she capitulated.

Begin again they did. After that first dance, Leigh spent the rest of the evening with Jason. She learned that he and his brother Bob, for whom Jason was deputizing tonight to escort Clare, farmed more than five hundred acres of land in central North Carolina, just over an hour's drive from Raleigh. He was persistent in his efforts to make her go out with him, saying he could drive to Raleigh from the farm whenever Leigh was free, so she laughingly gave in. She would have been inhuman not to, feeling Jason's magnetism as strongly as she did. He was charming and interesting and before the night was over Leigh was bemused.

He courted her assiduously. The Judge and Flora were almost as captivated by him as Leigh who had completely lost her heart. The one flaw in her happiness was an uncertainty of herself. She could not understand what a man like Jason, worldly and confident, could see in her, little more than a schoolgirl. She feared that she would be unable to hold his interest for long. He was tender and protective toward her, and teased her gently. But he was always in control, never carried away by their kisses, always able to put her aside and say good night. There was a part of him she couldn't reach. But when he asked her to marry him, she said yes at once. If he wanted her enough to marry her, he must love her, Leigh felt, so she stilled her doubts and told herself it would work out.

They were married three months after the Ball in the garden at Leigh's home. It was early spring and the weather was chancy, but Leigh insisted that the ceremony be held out of doors. She was right to do so. The day was beautiful and sunshiny, as only certain spring days can be, a gift after the cold of winter.

After a small reception for the few close friends they had invited, Leigh slipped away to change into her going-away clothes. Clare, her new sister-in-law, went with her. Leigh was floating with happiness and knew she needed someone to hold her down to earth long enough for her to change out of her wedding dress.

Clare quickly brought her back to reality.

As she was unfastening the tiny buttons down the back of Leigh's white lace gown, Clare spoke, "I like you, Leigh, and I'm glad we're going to be sisters."

Leigh was touched. She had met Clare only at the Ball and barely knew her. "Thank you, Clare. I'm glad, too."

Clare finished unbuttoning the dress and lifted it over Leigh's head. Then she took the gown to the closet and carefully hung it up.

"I don't quite know how to say this, but I'd like to give you some advice," she said as she moved to sit on a white and gold Louis XV chair.

Leigh hadn't expected such an offer. She

peeled off her white satin shoes and long silk slip before answering. She didn't want any advice, however well meant. Trying to joke, she said, "If it's the birds and bees, Clare, I know all about them."

"I'm serious," the other girl said tersely.

Resigned, Leigh shrugged. "All right, what is it?"

Clare watched Leigh don delicate underwear and reach for the pale blue wool dress lying in readiness on the bed. "It's about your behavior with Jason. You act so naïve and wide-eyed with him. He isn't going to put up with that for long."

Leigh stiffened. "Jason has never complained of my behavior, Clare," she said. "He must like me as I am or he wouldn't have married me."

Clare fidgeted with her gloves as Leigh sat down at the dressing table to touch up her makeup. "You think I'm interfering in something that doesn't concern me, don't you? It's just that I don't want to see you being taken advantage of. I'm going to tell you something that I think you ought to know."

Quietly Leigh asked, "Exactly what is it that you're trying to say?"

Upset and nervous, Clare jerked out the words, "Didn't you ever consider it strange that Jason took one look at you and practically proposed on the spot? Do you think that's what usually happens?"

"In some cases," Leigh answered, "people know right away, love at first sight does exist."

Her eyebrows drawn together in a frown, Clare chided, "Oh, come on, Leigh, be realistic. Does Jason strike you as the impulsive type? Do you know how many women have been in his life?"

Leigh didn't answer, just sat looking at Clare through the mirror.

"Jason decided before he escorted me to the Governor's Ball that he was going to choose a wife there. It didn't much matter whom, just someone pleasant to look at, with the right background—proper schools and family— and of course, most important, someone young enough to be malleable."

Leigh carefully put down the tube of lipstick she had been holding and said, "You don't know what you're talking about."

Rising from her chair, Clare moved restlessly around the room. "My husband Bob isn't a farmer," she explained. "He's been farming and hating every minute of it since his and Jason's father died two years ago. Bob had just taken a graduate degree from the State University, not in agriculture like Jason, but in engineering. Bob has always wanted to travel and build things. Jason is the elder, he was the one to take over the farm. But when Mr. Randall died, everything was in such confusion that Bob scrapped his plans and stayed to help out. He didn't want to leave Jason alone. But he's discontented at the farm and Jason knows it. So Jason decided that if he got married, he could convince Bob to leave to take up his career without feeling guilty."

Clenching her fists to keep herself from striking out at Clare, Leigh spoke, "I don't know why you're telling me this, Clare, but it simply is not true. Jason has too much integrity to marry for a cold-blooded purpose like that."

Clare answered with conviction. "Yes, Jason has principles, but you know as well as I do that he can be ruthless when something is important to him. He cares about Bob and wants him to be happy." She looked pityingly at Leigh. "I thought you should know."

Leigh was shaking. "I don't believe you," she said. "If Jason wanted Bob to go back to engineering, he could make him do so without resorting to a foolish marriage."

"Very well," Clare said angrily, "you've had an answer to everything I've told you. Go ahead, close your eyes to the truth if you can. Love is blind, they say." She paused deliberately before she made her final charge. "By the way, you won't be going to—where was it?—Venice on your honeymoon. Jason has canceled those plans, if he ever really intended to carry them out. He'll be taking you straight back to the farm today so that Bob and I can leave. Bob has accepted a job in Peru, building a bridge."

Leigh stood up, holding hard to her control. "Please leave this room, Clare. I don't want to hear any more." She felt sick and frightened.

When Clare had gone, Leigh pulled herself together and continued to prepare for her wedding trip, pretending that nothing had happened. She ignored the voice in the back of her head repeating what Clare had said. She dismissed the girl as a troublemaker, one of those people who can't bear to see others happy.

Moments later, Jason tapped lightly at the

door and walked into the room. He came to Leigh and kissed her. "Hello, Mrs. Randall."

Leigh smiled, her fears evaporating at the sight of him. "I'm almost ready. Are we running late?"

Jason put an arm around her shoulders. "I wanted to talk to you. Our plans have changed, Leigh. We won't be able to go away as we had planned. I didn't have a chance to tell you before, but something has come up at the farm that necessitates my returning there. As soon as the problem is cleared up, we'll have our honeymoon trip. You won't mind a delay, will you?"

Leigh stood very still, willing herself to behave normally.

She felt betrayed. "As a matter of fact, I do," she finally answered. Her voice seemed to come from somewhere outside the confusion in her head. She pushed away hysteria, trying to think. "Particularly, as I now realize that I am just a pawn in your family's schemes."

"What on earth are you talking about?" Jason demanded. His tone was enraged and Leigh faltered beneath his snapping, dark eyes.

"You always knew," she said slowly, "that we were never going to Venice, or, for that matter, that we were never going beyond your beloved farm. Why did you pretend anything else?"

Her voice faltered as Jason advanced and roughly seized her arm. "You silly little fool!" he said. "I should have known from the beginning that you were not interested in marrying a simple farmer! All you ever cared about was going to parties and flirting with the boys! I should have known better than to have married a society

26

beauty! Especially since I could see for myself that the Judge had spoiled you rotten! The only reason that you married me was because I was a challenge to your childish vanity—and the fact that I was the first man who would not take no for an answer."

Leigh wrenched away her arm, bruised by the encircling fingers of steel. His words seemed to confirm what Clare had told her. She walked over to the bed where her white picture hat lay, the bridal hat that she had donned so happily a few hours earlier. She was silent for a few painful moments, trying to regain her composure. Her quiet, happy childhood with the Judge and Flora had in no way prepared her for this dark, angry man.

Finally, she turned to face him. "If our plans have changed," she spoke quietly, "I guess I had better repack my bags." She bit her lip. "Things appropriate for Venice will hardly do for the farm." Not looking at Jason, she asked, "Would you please find Flora and ask her to help me?"

"Very well," he said curtly. "But don't keep me waiting too long. I am not your indulgent grandfather." He turned on his heel and walked out, slamming the door behind him.

For a moment, Leigh felt nothing. She walked over to the window and stared vacantly out. Then her emotions overcame her and she buried her face in her hands. Why, oh why, had she ever become involved with such a man? He had never loved her but had only needed her to fit into his plans—plans that had nothing to do with her as a person. What she had taken for love had been merely desire—the natural response of an experienced, virile man to the all too eager response of a young and innocent girl.

There was a gentle knock on the door. "Miss Leigh, did you call me? Mr. Randall said you needed help."

It was Flora. Leigh stumbled blindly up to her and flung her arms around her.

"Why, Miss Leigh! What can be the matter? And on your wedding day, too!" She embraced the trembling, crying girl.

Grasping Flora's arm like a lifeline, Leigh spoke, blind panic edging into her voice. "Don't ask any questions, just listen. This marriage was a terrible mistake and I can't go through with it. I'm leaving. Tell the Judge not to worry and that I'll call him."

Shock froze on the housekeeper's face. "Miss Leigh, you can't. What about Mr. Randall, the guests downstairs?"

Going to her night table, Leigh rummaged in a drawer to find a pen and paper. "Mr. Randall will arrange matters to suit himself," she said bitterly, "just as he always has. I'll leave him this note telling him that the marriage was a mistake and that I'm going away. He can do what he wants about it." She folded the paper and placed it in an envelope, adding her wide gold wedding band and the diamond engagement ring. As she handed it to Flora she begged, "Go and check the hall for me. See if the coast is clear."

Flora stood her ground, prepared to argue. "You can't do this, Miss Leigh. I won't let you. You weren't brought up to sneak away like a thief in the night. You stay here and face it, whatever it is."

"I can't, Flora, not this time."

Leigh gripped Flora's arms and shook her gently. "Please, if you care about me, help me now. Jason doesn't love me, he married me for another reason. Please help me." Leigh's voice broke. Her control was slipping and she knew that she had to get out of the house and fast.

Flora gave in reluctantly. "I just hope you know what you're doing."

Assured by the housekeeper that no one was near the hallway, Leigh picked up her purse and darted down the stairs and out the front door. Outside, the taxi she had called was waiting and she was on her way.

Afterwards Leigh was never quite sure how she got through the rest of that day. Although her emotions were completely numb, her mind was functioning clearly. She went to the airport and took the first available flight for New York City. There she taxied from LaGuardia Airport to the first decent-looking hotel that she saw. When she at last reached the haven of an anonymous hotel room, she went completely to pieces. She locked the door and stayed in the room for two days, sick with misery, alternately sobbing and cursing Jason. Finally it was the anger against him that got her on her feet. The pain was as fierce and strong as ever, but the anger was stronger.

She got a job. It wasn't much of a job, selling cosmetics in a Fifth Avenue department store, but then she wasn't trained for anything. When she called him, the Judge asked her to come home but he understood her pride and determination to stand on her own two feet.

Leigh was lucky. One day, up to her perfume counter stepped Gretta Dunn, the older sister of one of Leigh's school friends. Gretta had been in New York for about a year, working as a secretary for a firm of public relations agents. Right away she took Leigh under her wing. She soon had her moved out of the hotel where she was living and into Gretta's own apartment; two Southern girls on their own in the big city had to stick together she maintained. Then she set about convincing Leigh that with her coloring and grace she was a natural to model. "You're willowy and tall," Gretta urged, "just the right combination."

Almost without realizing how it happened, Leigh found herself with a career. Gretta got her started with introductions to the right people in advertising, people Gretta knew from her office, so Leigh didn't have to pound the pavements as much as other prospective models. But she worked hard; it helped to lessen the agony she felt. Within a year she was established, her photographs appearing in all the right places. It always disconcerted her to pick up a glossy fashion magazine and see her own face staring back from its cover.

In time the pain and disillusionment of her disastrous marriage faded to a dull ache. It was almost as if it had never happened. She was busy and no one around her knew anything about her past. On his occasional visits to New

York the Judge never referred to her marriage. But Leigh didn't forget.

There were men in her life, of course. She was too beautiful for there not to be. She had dozens of men friends, and she went out frequently and had a good time. But there was no one she couldn't walk away from without a backward glance. When a relationship seemed to be getting serious, Leigh easily broke it off. She was the one in control, and she had no intention of becoming emotionally involved with anyone. She was aloof, cool and untouchable, and nothing could shake her. However, Leigh knew what no one else could even suspect, that deep inside she was terrified of being hurt again. She had a scar that would never fade and she hated Jason for inflicting it. But she had grown up. She was no longer the Judge's little granddaughter. She was a beautiful woman.

Chapter Two

"I'll get it," Leigh called out as the doorbell chimed. She paused to glance at herself in the mirror. Her reflection looked back at her, calm and assured. The simple black jersey dress she was wearing made her hair, falling straight to her shoulders from a center part, seem even more silvery by contrast. Leigh touched the strand of milky pearls at her throat, thinking sadly of the Judge who had given them to her on her eighteenth birthday.

She hurried down the stairs and opened the door. Jason stood there, tall, broad-shouldered and completely formidable in a well-tailored navy suit. After greeting him she led the way to the study and motioned him to a chair.

"May I get you some coffee or a drink?" she offered.

Jason remained standing, his face impassive. "Whiskey, please, if you have it."

"Yes, but I'll have to go to the kitchen for it. Everything is being packed up and most of the boxes are in there."

When Leigh returned a few minutes later, Jason was near the almost empty bookshelves, examining a leatherbound volume he held in his hand.

"I presume you're selling the house," he said without turning toward her. "What are you going to do with your grandfather's books?"

"Some of them I'll keep," Leigh answered as she handed Jason his drink. "The rest, especially the law books, will be donated to the Judge's university."

Leigh sat down in a blue Queen Anne wing chair and indicated its mate, across from her, to Jason.

No longer bothering to hide the contempt in his eyes, Jason looked her over assessingly as he lowered himself into the chair.

"It's been a long time, Leigh," he drawled. "You're even more beautiful than ever, if that's possible."

Leigh did not answer. Somehow the words hadn't sounded like a compliment.

"Successful, too, I hear," he commented.

Leigh realized that this interview was going to be even more difficult than she had expected. To take control of the situation she assumed a brisk, businesslike manner and plunged in, "Jason, what I wanted to talk to you about—" She floundered and tried again. "I, ah, would like arrangements to be made for a divorce or an annulment of our marriage."

"I wondered when you'd get around to that," he said, displaying no surprise at her statement.

"I didn't get in touch with you before because I was away and I didn't want the Judge to have to handle it for me. I guess I wanted to spare him any more notoriety."

Jason made a rude remark, and Leigh turned on him furiously. "Is it so inconceivable that I wanted to protect my grandfather from further hurt over my mistake?" she hissed.

Calmly sipping his drink, Jason gave her a hard look. "Don't hand me noble motives, Leigh," he said. "You've never thought of anyone but yourself in your whole life. The Judge certainly had to endure a considerable amount of unpleasantness when you walked out after the wedding. Who did you think would have to face all the guests you left behind? Or didn't you care?"

With a smooth motion he stood up and reached over to pull Leigh to her feet. He put his hand under her chin and lifted her face to the light, his touch burning her skin.

"Such a lovely, unawakened face," he said thoughtfully. Then his dark eyes bored into hers and Leigh knew that he was very angry indeed. "But we both know that you'd have to be far from innocent to get where you've gotten in the modeling business."

The insulting words completely shattered Leigh's mask of composure.

"You despicable—" Her hand shot up toward

Jason's face, but his was quicker, and her wrist was caught in a grip of steel.

"You'd better be glad I stopped you, lady, because I certainly would have hit you back," he ground out.

Leigh twisted her wrist from his grasp. She wanted to hurt him more than she had ever wanted anything in her life. Struggling to bring her runaway emotions under control, she went to lean against her grandfather's desk, running her hand absently along its smooth surface. After a moment she turned to face Jason and said, "I should think that you would want to end this farce of a marriage as much as I do. In fact, I'm surprised that you haven't contacted me about it." She tilted her head to look up at him. "I was sure that you would want a wife and family to help run that farm of yours." A short pause. "Or can't you find anybody willing to take you on, Jason?" she asked sweetly.

He smiled—not a nice smile. "Being unavailable for matrimony has its—ah—advantages. It helps my lady friends to know the score."

Leigh gasped at his effrontery. She moved restlessly around the room, at last coming to stand by her chair. "We aren't getting anywhere," she said quietly. "I don't want to swap insults with you, Jason. I just want to get this settled. Will you apply for the annulment or shall I?"

"You're a cool customer, aren't you, Leigh? You think you can waltz back here after five years and say 'jump, pretty please' and expect me to ask 'how high?' Ah, yes," he sneered, "by all means, let's tie up the loose ends—sell the house, shed a husband. It's a pity that you didn't bother to get to know me and what I wanted in a wife before you married me." His eyes, more black now than brown, scorched her face as the harsh words exploded from his mouth. "The joke was well and truly on me," he spat out, his fury bursting forth unrestrained. "I thought that you were just young, a little spoiled. In time, I felt, you would grow up and be able to handle a commitment, a real give-and-take relationship. But not you. You preferred make-believe, moonlight and roses. You had caught an eligible bachelor and you expected him to give you a glamorous social life, not responsibilities. Hard reality hit, didn't it, when I told you we'd have to postpone our honeymoon? Was it a shock to find out that I valued the farm so highly, Leigh?" His voice was biting and cruel. "The selfish little butterfly couldn't take it and ran away. I badly misjudged you, Leigh. I didn't learn until too late that there is no substance under that beautiful exterior. I believe superficial is the fitting description."

She felt bruised by his assault. She hadn't realized what construction he would put on her flight. How foolish not to know that Clare would never admit to being the spur that drove Leigh away. Well, Jason had a nerve to censure her. He had married her under false pretenses, hadn't he? He was equally at fault but she was not going to stand here and trade excuses with him. It was much too late for that.

With as much aplomb as she could muster,

Leigh answered, "I don't care what you think of me, Jason."

His return was quiet and deadly. "Don't expect me to make it easy for you, my dear. I'm not a forgiving man."

"I never thought you were," she said.

Leigh's breathing was constricted. Moving to the French windows, she opened one and stood pulling large gulps of fresh air into her lungs. She knew she couldn't take much more.

"All right, Jason," she conceded, standing by the window with her head down. "You have reason for being bitter just as I had reason for running away. But it's over, let it go." She sighed and lifted a hand as if in supplication. "I wanted to end the marriage officially while I was here in Raleigh. Can't you understand? I won't be coming back."

When he made no response, she said resignedly. "All right, have your revenge by refusing the annulment. I won't bother you about it anymore."

Her head flew up as Jason countered softly, "I didn't say I wouldn't agree to an annulment. I said I wouldn't make it easy for you."

Some of the fight was returning to Leigh. "What are you talking about?" she asked suspiciously.

It was Jason's turn to prowl the room. After a long silence, he motioned to the wing chairs and told Leigh to sit down.

"I have a proposition to put to you," he added, a look of speculation on his dark face. "I want a few months of your time."

Leigh had hunched herself in the chair, but at Jason's words she jerked upright like a puppet on a string. She examined his face for signs of derision but encountered only hard brown eyes staring into her gray ones. He was serious. Immediately Leigh raised her guard higher. Somehow she knew that she wasn't going to like what was coming.

"Would you please explain?" she asked.

Jason settled back in his chair and looked her over. "It's not what you're thinking. I don't have any designs on your—ah—virtue. You lost your attraction for me five years ago. At the very least I have to like something about the woman I take to my bed."

For the first time in years, Leigh blushed.

Ignoring her discomfiture, Jason continued, "I'd like to make a business arrangement with you, a *quid pro quo*. You scratch my back and I'll scratch yours, figuratively speaking, of course." After a slight hesitation he asked, "Do you remember my brother Bob and his wife Clare?"

As he spoke those names, Leigh stiffened. She gripped her hands together so hard that the nails were piercing her flesh and stared speechlessly back at Jason.

"They're in Brazil," he said. "Bob was supervising the construction of a building last week when a part of it collapsed and he was trapped by a steel girder. By the time he was extricated his leg was badly mangled. He's in traction in a Rio hospital and can't be moved for at least two months, maybe more."

"I'm sorry, Jason. I hope that Bob will be all

right, but I can't see what his accident has to do with me," Leigh returned uncertainly.

"You would if you'd let me finish," Jason shot back. "Bob and Clare have a three-year-old daughter, Jody. She and Clare were here, in North Carolina, when the accident happened. They had been with Bob, but since he was working night and day to bring the project in on time, Clare and Jody returned ahead of him. He was due for leave soon. Anyway, when we were notified about Bob's injury, Clare naturally flew to Rio, leaving Jody with me." The brown eyes narrowed. "Do you begin to understand my problem?"

Leigh had a horrible idea that she did. In a halting voice she asked, "Who's taking care of Jody?"

"My cousin, but she's also my housekeeper and can't watch Jody and take care of her own job at the same time. Aside from running the house, just now she has extra work because of spring planting. She's been managing so far, but she can't possibly keep it up for two months."

"And you have me in mind for baby-sitter?"

"Yes. Will you do it?"

Leigh's nerves were beginning to shriek. Spend two months near Jason—impossible! And the thought of taking care of Clare's child was repugnant. Maybe Clare had done her a favor by revealing why Jason had married her, but Leigh felt only distaste when she thought of the woman. She forced herself to speak slowly and clearly. "Jason, I'm sorry for your plight, but if you think I could be a substitute mother, you're out of your mind."

"Why?"

Trying to remain calm, Leigh enumerated, "First, there's my career. I have commitments. I only came to Raleigh for a few days. I have to get back to New York. A model doesn't just take off for several months at a time. I worked hard to get where I am, Jason. A few months away and I could be forgotten."

"Who could forget you, Leigh?" Jason asked dryly.

She ignored him. "Also, I know absolutely nothing about children. I've never been around them. They scare me silly. I honestly wouldn't know what to do for Jody," she pleaded.

"It can't be so hard," he replied. "New mothers take care of their infants every day. You're a smart girl, Leigh, you'll learn."

She tried again. "I'm sorry, Jason, but I just can't take this on. You'll have to find someone else."

"Will I?" he questioned. "Did I forget to mention that if you do this small favor for me, I'll initiate proceedings for an annulment immediately?" He smiled unpleasantly and Leigh felt very apprehensive suddenly.

"However, if you turn me down, I might be forced to sue for divorce, charging you with desertion and anything else I can think up. I don't think that you will find me an easy opponent. I assure you that I can make life quite unpleasant for you. I have spoken to Mr. Judkins, and he is quite willing to take on the case. Don't forget, my dear, that we are not as lenient about those things here as are your sophisticated city friends."

Leigh was stunned. "You wouldn't be so petty!"

"Try me and see," he taunted. And then, almost as if speaking to himself, he added, "I don't know which prospect intrigues me more, the joy of engaging in a first-class court fight with you or that of seeing the cool, society beauty struggling with a three-year-old."

Leigh believed him. He was ruthless enough to try anything. She was all too well aware of Mr. Judkins's reputation. His divorce cases had been smeared all over the gossip columns when she was growing up in Raleigh. The intimate details had been there for all to read about and snicker over. Her face flamed. Who knows what crazy statements Jason would make about her? She had felt the full force of his anger before and she knew that, even with the experience and sophistication that she had learned over those years working in the city, she still did not want to take Jason on in public. It was not only that she was afraid of this bitter, angry man, but more important, she was too proud. She could feel her old wound throbbing beneath the scar. She did not want to open it again for all to see it gaping.

"You win," she said, pressing her lips tightly together to control their trembling. "You must want to punish me very much."

Jason stood, his eyes full of bitterness. "You don't know how much."

As she walked him to the door, he told her that he would pick her up on Friday morning to go to the farm. "Be ready," he warned before he left.

Leigh slammed the door hard behind him and

stood pounding the flat of her hand impotently against the wood, railing against his invincibility. She had always known that Jason would make a dangerous and implacable enemy, and he was her enemy now. What was worse, she had just delivered herself into his hands. He intended to make her pay in full for walking out on him. Well, she had a score to settle too. He had won this round, but maybe, just maybe, she wasn't beaten yet.

Leigh tilted her chin and marched into the kitchen to break the disastrous news to Flora.

Silence reigned in the car. Jason, concentrating on the road, seemed preoccupied, and Leigh was busy fighting back the apprehension that welled up in her at the thought of the next two months. She had tried looking out the window, but the repetition of trees and billboards couldn't hold her interest, centered as it was on the driver of the car. Her awareness of him was almost a tangible thing, and she hated it. With a sigh, she lay her head against the back of the seat, relieved at least that Jason drove such a luxurious car. Leigh was tired. She hadn't been sleeping well and the last two days had been frantic— packing, convincing her agent that she needed a few months off, closing the house. Putting Flora on the bus to Wilmington had been the worst; it was like saying good-bye to the last remnants of her girlhood.

Leigh started out of her half-doze when she felt the car turning off the expressway.

"Just another twenty minutes or so," Jason

said, slanting her a sardonic glance. "I'm sure you can't wait to get there."

Without answering she rolled down her window and peered out. The car was passing through a small, rather stark town, its one main street lined with shops. Leigh hadn't visited this part of North Carolina before, but she could guess that this town existed solely to supply the needs of the surrounding farmers. From studying North Carolina history at school she knew that the central part of the state, the Piedmont, was primarily rural. An anachronism, she thought, picturing in her mind the urban sprawl so familiar in New York. Here was preserved something of the country as it must have been in the nineteenth century, when most of the United States was rural and industrialization was in its infancy. Maybe she would enjoy this forced exile, Leigh decided, because she would definitely be getting back to nature.

As the town was left behind, houses became farther and farther apart, most of them bordered by outbuildings and wide fields plowed ready for planting. Leigh liked the barns particularly, many weathered and dilapidated, but some covered in bright patchwork squares of a metallic material that glinted in the weak April sunshine.

"Jason, what do they grow here?" she asked, deciding that she needed some information if she was to be here for a while.

"Tobacco, mostly," he told her. "It's the most lucrative crop, but the government keeps a tight control over how much can be grown by giving the farmers allotments. Still, the profits from a summer crop of tobacco are enough to get many farmers through the winter."

He took one hand from the wheel and gestured toward the passing fields. "Lots of other things grow well too because of the rich soil. Let's see—corn, beans, peas, sweet potatoes, tomatoes, all kinds of vegetables and fruits."

"Is that what you grow?"

Jason turned to look at her, a cynical expression on his face. "Why the sudden interest? You never bothered to ask before. You never even so much as visited the farm," he accused.

Leigh's mouth went dry. "You know that there wasn't really time, everything happened in such a whirlwind with us. I was in school, you were coming to see me weekends. We were trying to get to know each other."

"We didn't do a very good job, did we," Jason commented.

Leigh sighed and shifted uneasily in her seat. After a few minutes she tried again. "Well, what do you grow? I really am interested."

"All the things every other farmer around here grows. Tobacco and vegetables in the summer, peanuts and fruits in the autumn," Jason recited.

A puzzled expression on her face, Leigh asked, "What do you do in the winter if your crops are finished in the autumn?"

"I have a few sidelines," Jason explained. "Farming doesn't take up much of my time, Leigh. A good manager and tenant farmers free me to pursue other interests." He paused, then said softly, "It's difficult to make much money in farming these days, so I diversified. I had to be able to afford someone like you, honey."

Determined to keep things as harmonious as possible, Leigh ignored the jibe and waited for him to continue.

"Harrellsville, about ten miles away from the farm, is where most of my other ventures are located. I have a cannery where products from my farm and neighboring farms are preserved, and a long-distance trucking operation which distributes the canned goods."

Leigh was mildly shocked. She hadn't realized that Jason's undertakings were quite so extensive.

Suddenly he braked and turned into a narrow road lined with oak trees. Meadows and fields, geometrically bounded by rail fencing, stretched as far as the eye could see.

"Is this yours?" asked Leigh.

Jason nodded and pointed out the window. "This land has been in my family for generations, long before the Civil War. We almost lost it once." He quirked an eyebrow at Leigh as if to question her attention. At her nod he went on with the tale.

"My grandfather and his four brothers were each willed one hundred acres of land when their father died, thus breaking up the original five hundred acre holding. The property was further fragmented when three of the brothers sold their portions to move into town. Times were hard and farming was a tough way to make a living. The fourth brother died and his property was divided among various heirs, so eventually my grandfather was the only one left, and his dream was to restore the property to its original size. He was a determined man."

Jason gazed far into the distance as if seeing into the past.

"When the Depression came in 1929, the price of land fell drastically. My grandfather had a little money saved; he didn't trust banks so he kept his savings in a strongbox in the house and thus didn't lose it when the banks failed. Little by little he bought back the land, a whole farm or an acre or two at a time. It must have been a laborious process. He used to brag that at one time, when things were at their bleakest, he paid only fifteen cents an acre. He eventually recovered the entire property."

As Leigh watched Jason's rugged face, she knew that he had inherited his grandfather's stubbornness and determination along with the five hundred acres.

Jason slowed the car. "We're here," he announced.

The fields had given way to a wide sloping lawn, emerald green and smooth. Crowning a small rise of land in the center of that carpet of green stood the most interesting house that Leigh had ever seen. It wasn't the most beautiful because of its irregularities. She uttered a soft sigh. This would have been her home if things had worked out differently. Sensing that Jason was waiting for a comment, she told him, "It's lovely. Quite, quite lovely."

Of white frame with black shutters, the house had obviously started out, many years ago, as a classically balanced dwelling, its severity softened by huge old boxwoods and masses of flowers. Several additions had been made, not wings exactly but rambling extensions, linked together by a long, shaded porch. Rather than hodgepodge, as one would expect, each addition added character to the house and the total effect was charming.

Jason brought the car to a halt near the front door and before Leigh could climb out tossed a small box in her lap, saying casually, "Better wear those. Folks around here are conventional."

Leigh lifted the lid to reveal her wedding and engagement rings which she awkwardly pushed onto her finger.

As they stepped onto the porch, Leigh shaking the wrinkles from her green knit dress, the front door opened and a tall, angular woman in bright pink stepped out. Quirking her lips into what seemed to be a smile, she spoke to Jason tartly. "It's time you were back. Took long enough."

Then she looked Leigh over, strong disapproval in her eyes. "This must be your wife."

Jason introduced Leigh to his cousin, Mary Smith, or Smitty as he said everyone called her.

The woman's answer was an inelegant "humph." She ignored Leigh's greeting and led the way inside the shining oak-floored hall, telling Jason over her shoulder that she would fetch the child.

Before she could reach the curving staircase, he had halted her with a hand on her arm. "What about some coffee first, Smitty? We've had a long drive."

Smitty turned around and disappeared through a door at the back of the hall.

"I gather she's upset because I'm here," Leigh commented.

Not bothering to deny her guess, Jason directed Leigh toward the double doors on the right side of the hall. Entering the living room she gazed around in wonder. Done in shades of green and gold, the room looked both elegant and comfortable, not a usual combination. And much-used, Leigh thought, noticing that the couch and several deep armchairs were arranged around a table scattered with magazines, and that a book lay open on the stool of the grand piano in the corner.

Jason was watching as she sank into the depths of the gold velvet couch. "The room suits you," he declared surprisingly.

Embarrassed and ill at ease, Leigh was glad when Smitty appeared with a loaded tray.

As they sipped their coffee, the silence lengthened.

"Do you live here alone?" Leigh asked abruptly in an attempt to relieve the tension she felt.

Jason raised black eyebrows. "Curious about my domestic arrangements, Leigh?" he drawled.

Choking on the hot coffee, she spluttered, "I was just trying to make civil conversation and you know it."

There was a slight pause before Jason replied. "Yes, I live here alone, except when Bob and Clare are between assignments." He added coolly, "My nights aren't lonely, though, if that's what you wanted to know."

Leigh's cup clattered into the saucer just as Jason rose from his chair. "We'll get some air while we wait for Smitty," he said, taking Leigh's elbow to guide her to the door.

Leigh pulled violently away from him. His touch was disturbing. "Keep your hands off me, Jason," she hissed.

"With pleasure, my dear," he said smoothly and led the way to the back of the house, through a pleasantly cluttered sun-room, and outside to a slate patio.

It was a lovely spot. Flowering pink and white dogwood trees were clustered around the patio and beyond it, visible through the trees, a kidney-shaped pool was under construction, being built from the same stone as the patio. Before Leigh had had more than a cursory glance around, Smitty was calling them to come inside the house.

In the hall Smitty was holding the hand of a plump little girl dressed in a blue pinafore, her shining brown hair pulled into a fat sausage curl on top of her head.

When she caught sight of Jason she ran to him, reaching up her arms to be held. He swung her up in his arms for a few seconds before depositing her again on her own two feet.

"Jody, I want you to meet your Aunt Leigh," he said. "She's going to be taking care of you for a while."

Jody turned a serious round face to Leigh, held out her hand, and said hello. Kneeling down until she was Jody's height, Leigh took the outstretched hand and as solemnly greeted the little girl. She didn't really know what to say to the child.

Suddenly Jody gave her a mischievous grin

that reminded Leigh forcibly of Jason. *If she's like her uncle*, thought Leigh, her heart skipping a beat, *then I'm in for more trouble*.

Jason took Jody's hand and led her toward the front door. "Come on, Leigh, we'd better get going."

"Get going where?" Leigh asked, not moving. "I was under the impression that this is your house."

Jason turned to her, his voice silky. "Didn't I tell you? We won't be staying here. I'm having some remodeling done, a noisy business."

Leigh didn't trust him an inch. "From what I saw, the pool is far enough from the house for the workmen not to make too big a disturbance."

"Ah, but the pool is only the beginning. Next come the upstairs rooms. Hammering, sawing, clutter and dust. It would be too unsettling for a hothouse flower like you, my dear. Now Smitty here is tough as old shoe leather. Nothing bothers her, but you and Jody will be better off away from all the upheaval."

He raised a hand to ward off the protests she was struggling to make. "I've got just the place for us. Exactly what you need, Leigh, a quiet, little cottage. Come on." And with that he firmly herded Leigh and the child out to the car.

After Jody's luggage was stowed in the trunk, the child was installed in the back seat and Leigh in front and Jason drove swiftly down a road that curved around the house and its outbuildings. He passed two cottages standing close together and motioned to them without slowing.

"A couple of my tenant farmers live there," he

volunteered. "You'll be able to walk down to visit them from our place."

Another mile or so and Jason pulled into the driveway of a small, square house, similar to the ones they had passed except that this one did not have the well cared for appearance of the other two. It badly needed painting and the yard was unkempt, filled with weeds and more bald spots than grass. Jason helped Leigh out of the car and swept her a mocking bow.

"Welcome to your new home."

Chapter Three

Leigh was speechless.

"What's the matter, my dear? Not grand enough for you?" Jason asked with a harsh laugh.

Suddenly Leigh was beginning to comprehend just what he had in mind for her.

Jason took her elbow, his touch sending a tingle along her nerve ends. "Come along. I'm sure you can't wait to see the rest of it."

The interior of the house looked just like the outside, neglected and unkempt. As Jason ushered her in, Leigh stifled a wild impulse to turn around and run as fast as she could in the opposite direction.

Holding Jody by the hand, Jason showed her around, carelessly explaining that the house until recently had been occupied by one of his farm workers who had since moved on. "A bachelor, who didn't much care about housework," he added unnecessarily.

The front door opened directly into a large room which ran the width of the house. It was apparently used for a dining room as well as a living room, as evidenced by a round oak table and four high-backed chairs pushed into a corner. The rest of the furnishings were sparse: a sofa and chair that had seen better days, several small tables and an empty bookcase. The once-varnished pine floor was partially covered by a worn brown rug that somehow fit in with the mottled walls.

Aware that Jason was watching closely for her reaction, Leigh carefully kept her face devoid of expression.

Down a short hallway that opened off one end of the room were two bedrooms with a bath in between.

"Mine," Jason said succinctly, indicating the first door. Walking to the second one, he pushed it open and pointed to the single bed and crib that the room contained.

"You and Jody will share in here." His well-cut mouth quirked at one corner. "It seemed the best arrangement."

Jody dived for a doll propped up against a box of blocks in the corner. Jason explained that Jody's clothes had been transferred, along with the toys, from the other house.

Twisting the strap of her tan leather shoulder bag, Leigh hesitantly voiced her thoughts. "There's really no need for you to stay here, Jason. Jody and I will manage, I'm sure," she asserted with more confidence than she felt.

He gave her a cold look. "I'm sure that you could, Leigh, but that's not the point of my staying here. This cottage is rather isolated, there are no neighbors within shouting distance and there is no telephone. Jody was left in my care, and I intend to see to it that no harm comes to her. I won't be around much if that's what's bothering you."

Leigh shivered at the ice in his tones.

He motioned her into the kitchen just across the hall, leaving Jody happily cuddling her doll. Rather hurriedly, Jason gave her a general idea of the kitchen layout and mentioned that Smitty had stocked up on food for them.

"I'll get your bags," he said on his way through the door. "There should be something warming in the oven for lunch."

Leigh made a face at the retreating back. "I guess that means I'm supposed to dish it up," she murmured to herself as she gave the room a closer inspection than Jason's disturbing presence had heretofore allowed her. If anything, it was worse than the main room. Here the walls had gone beyond being mottled. What had once been a flowered wallpaper was now peeling in places. The floor seemed to be covered with some sort of linoleum, long since faded to an indiscriminate grayish tone.

Obviously Jason intended to make her stay here as uncomfortable as possible as some sort of perverted retribution for the blow she had dealt his pride. Well, she had given her word, so she was stuck here, but she wasn't going to give Jason the satisfaction of moaning about it, Leigh decided with spirit as she bent to peek in the oven.

He probably expected the luxury-loving fashion model to bolt at the first sight of this place, Leigh told herself, grinning. Oh, if he only knew. She got good commissions for her modeling jobs now that she was sought after by the top magazines, but it hadn't always been that way. In fact, when she was just starting out, she had had quite a struggle, a hand-to-mouth existence for a while. She had refused financial help from her grandfather, determined to make it on her own, and she had. Her present apartment was quite cozy, but the first one that she could manage, without a roommate, had been one room with a hotplate for a kitchen and the bathroom down the hall.

Opening a few cupboards to find dishes and cutlery, Leigh quickly set the formica-topped table for three, noting that someone had brought a booster seat for Jody. She was just putting a steaming chicken casserole on a mat in the center of the table when Jason came in, carrying a giggling Jody piggyback. He had discarded his gray suit for a plaid shirt and well-worn jeans, which closely molded his lean form. Not a spare ounce of flesh on him, Leigh thought as she watched the powerful shoulders flex when he swung Jody into her chair.

Not wanting to be caught observing him, Leigh turned to the counter to slice the loaf of bread Smitty had provided.

During lunch, Jason briefed her on Jody's routine and Leigh listened carefully. Never having taken care of a child before, she felt she needed all the pointers she could get.

"How do you like the cottage?" Jason asked slyly, suddenly changing the subject.

"Oh, it's not too bad," Leigh answered cheerfully.

A look of ill-concealed surprise flitted across Jason's strong features. Clearly her response was not what he had expected.

"It reminds me of my first apartment on my own," she continued, a gleam of mischief in the clear gray eyes. "Of course," she tilted her head consideringly, "this cottage is much larger than my place was."

His only answer was a skeptical glance, the black eyebrows raised in disbelief.

Leigh couldn't help adding with wide-eyed innocence. "I'm pretty handy with a paintbrush and a needle. Maybe you'd like me to fix the cottage up a bit for your next tenant while I'm here."

With a frown, Jason pushed back his chair and stood up.

"I have work to do. If you need help for any reason while I'm away, there's a bell hanging on a pole by the back door. Ring it. Around here, that signals emergency."

He went to give Jody a kiss, telling her to be a good girl for her Auntie Leigh. Watching him, Leigh marveled at the tender expression on his usually cold face.

"I should be back around dinnertime," was his farewell to her as he disappeared from view.

Rather unsure of herself, Leigh approached Jody who was staring solemnly back at her, and

56

tentatively held out a hand to help the child down from the table.

"Uncle Jason says you have a nap after lunch, Jody. Would you like me to read you a story first?" she offered.

The little girl nodded and led the way into the bedroom they were to share. In no time at all, Leigh had her tucked in, her teddy bear caught tightly under her arm.

Poor little tyke, Leigh thought as she made her way back to the kitchen. It must be unsettling to be thrust into the care of a complete stranger.

After the dishes were done, Leigh tiptoed back into the bedroom to check on the child. She was sleeping peacefully, the rather scruffy-looking bear still clutched to her. What an angel, Leigh thought at the sight of the brown curls tumbled on the pillow and the fat little cheeks rosy with sleep. Maybe these weeks wouldn't be so bad after all, with Jody as compensation.

Actually, Leigh hadn't had a break from her job in several years. Every time she decided to take a few weeks off, some big assignment would come her way and Dan, her agent, would insist that she take it and defer the vacation.

As quietly as possible, so she wouldn't disturb Jody, Leigh changed her tailored green dress for jeans and a yellow T-shirt. The jeans were old and tight, left over from Leigh's school days, but they were the only ones she had with her so they would have to do. Coming to Raleigh at a moment's notice to attend the funeral, Leigh hadn't brought much in the way of clothes with her. She unpacked the meager wardrobe, hanging the dresses in the closet and putting the small supply of underclothes in a dresser drawer. Maybe she would be able to buy a few necessities in the nearest town.

Peering into the mirror atop the dresser, Leigh pulled her blond hair tightly back into a high ponytail and grimaced at the reflection that looked back at her. What she did not realize was that the severity of the style suited her, emphasizing her high cheekbones and revealing what her softly swinging shoulder-length tresses often hid, a rounded but very determined chin.

Leigh spent the time until Jody awoke wandering around the cottage, trying to determine what she could do to make it more habitable. It would serve Jason right if she left everything as it was, but with Jody living here, she would clean the place up. The one room she didn't go into was Jason's. Just the realization that she had to see him every day and go on seeing him made her nervous enough without dwelling on their enforced intimacy in the small cottage. She had loved him, but she had gotten over him. In New York, as time passed, she was able to banish him from her mind. Here, it was going to be much more difficult. One thing she hadn't forgotten was the physical response he had aroused in her, a burning passion she had never since felt for any other man. If he ever touched her again, she promised herself she would scream the house down. Not that there was much likelihood. He had made it crystal clear what he thought of her.

Leigh's chaotic thoughts were disturbed by a small cry that had her rushing into Jody's room. The child was in the process of climbing over the rails of the crib. Leigh went to give her a hand and led her off to the bathroom.

Jody seemed to be a reserved, quiet child. Although Leigh admittedly didn't know much about children and what made them tick, she had a lot of common sense and realized she should take things slowly with Jody. She was the stranger, the newcomer in Jody's life, and she would have to be patient until Jody was ready to accept her.

The rest of the afternoon went well. They took a companionable walk in the woods behind the cottage, stopping frequently to examine budding flowers or to pick up interesting rocks and bits of moss. Jody was more vocal than she had been before and ran about uninhibitedly, especially when a brightly colored butterfly teased her to chase it. On the way back to the cottage she slipped her hand shyly into Leigh's.

After the walk, Leigh suggested a bath and Jody agreed, albeit reluctantly, and then proceeded to enjoy herself thoroughly. She splashed so much that by the time Leigh lifted her out of the tub, Leigh was half-soaked, the yellow T-shirt clinging to her like a second skin.

She was enfolding Jody in a big, soft towel when she noticed Jason leaning negligently in the doorway, making the small room seem much smaller.

"Which one of you had the bath?"

"Very funny," muttered Leigh, self-conscious in the revealing shirt and tight jeans, aware of how Jason's eyes were moving over her.

He offered to dress Jody in the pajamas lying ready on a bathroom shelf, and Leigh escaped to the bedroom to change back into the green dress. Its tailored simplicity molded her willowy form, and the almond color was reflected in her eyes, deepening them. She was just brushing out her hair when Jason tapped lightly on the door before walking in.

He took in the green dress and lifted a mocking eyebrow. "Are you more comfortable now?"

Leigh was far from comfortable in his disturbing presence. "More presentable, at least," she answered.

Leisurely he looked her up and down. "Oh, I wouldn't say that," he drawled. "I rather liked you as you were."

Annoyed at his baiting, Leigh brushed past and went into the kitchen.

There, she rummaged in the refrigerator to find the two thick steaks she had spotted earlier. She seasoned them lightly and put them under the broiler. Uncertain about what Jody would eat, she boiled two eggs and got out a box of cornflakes, just in case. By the time she had assembled a salad and set the table, everything was ready.

Jason concentrated on Jody during the meal, asking her questions about how she had spent the afternoon. It was only when Leigh got up to clear the table that he turned his attention to her.

"I think it's time we had a talk, Leigh," he said as he scooped Jody up. "When you've finished in here." It was an order.

While Jason was settling Jody for the night, Leigh turned on the electric percolator and set out a tray with cups, sugar and cream. Suddenly Jason called to her.

"Jody wants you to come and say good night."

Touched more than she could have imagined, Leigh bent over the little girl. As she lifted her head and saw Jason adjust the lightweight blanket covering the child, Leigh was struck by the poignancy of the moment. If she and Jason had not parted on their wedding day, this could have been their own daughter they were tucking in. Shaken, Leigh hurried out of the room.

They carried their coffee into the living room and drank it in silence. Finally Jason put his empty cup on the tray and leaned back on the sofa, supremely at ease, his long legs stretched out in front of him.

"You've changed, Leigh," he said at last, his dark eyes boring into her as if trying to fathom her depths. "At first I thought it was just the elegant clothes, but it's more than that."

"You mean I don't hang on your every word and gaze adoringly at you anymore," she answered flippantly.

"Did you ever do that?"

"That was why you married me, wasn't it? I was so biddable." A trace of bitterness was discernible in Leigh's usually sweet voice.

Jason continued to study her. "Why did you run away?" he asked after a long moment.

"Because I found out why you married me."

"And why was that?"

"You needed a wife and I happened to be available."

The dark eyes narrowed. His face was a cold, hard mask, and he did not deny her words.

"You should have made it clearer to me that you were marrying me for convenience," she burst out, wanting to hit at him, to make a dent in the wall of his composure. "I was young, remember. I stupidly assumed you loved me."

"I never lied to you, Leigh."

"How about by omission? By neglecting to inform me of the particulars of our marriage. How your feelings, love, didn't enter into it on your part."

"Love!" He spat out the word. "What's that? You can't base marriage on misguided emotion."

Agitatedly Leigh pushed a strand of silky silver hair behind her ear. He was a cold-blooded, inhuman machine and she loathed him.

He read the emotions playing across her face and disregarded them.

"The marriage could have worked, Leigh. You should have given it a chance."

Her head drooped, as if her slender neck were too frail to hold it. Then she looked up, straight into his accusing eyes.

"I'm not proud of what I did. I know I took the coward's way out, running away instead of facing you. But it wouldn't have changed anything, you know."

Briefly she closed her eyes. "I did write to you, to explain."

"Ah, yes, your letter. It merely confirmed my conviction that I had had a narrow escape. A polite little note saying you had made a mistake. What you really meant was that you couldn't stand to live on a farm, away from the bright lights."

"It wasn't that at all. I've tried to tell you . . ." Her voice faded. She knew he wouldn't believe her anyway.

"Was it bad for you after the wedding?" She ventured to ask something that had long been bothering her. "I mean, did everyone here know?"

"That I'd been jilted? No. Since the wedding was to be a small one, I had only told my brother and his wife and Smitty. There was no big announcement, so don't worry, you won't have to face a lot of awkward questions. As far as everyone around here is concerned, we're newlyweds."

"I didn't mean—oh, what's the use? We're on different wavelengths."

Leigh had been genuinely concerned about the humiliation he might have suffered at her hands, on returning home without a bride, but he would never accept that. She didn't seem to be able to break through the wall of misconceptions he had formed against her, but maybe it was best not even to try.

Getting restlessly to her feet, Leigh walked over to the window to gaze without seeing into the darkness outside. The mingled fragrance of sweet spring flowers that wafted in through the half-opened window was an incongruous accompaniment to the tense atmosphere in the room. Leigh reached up and pulled down the sash.

"Look, Jason," she said, turning around, "I'm here. I've agreed to stay until Jody's parents return. Can't we leave it at that and let the past rest in peace? We'll be getting the annulment soon anyway."

"Is there a man, Leigh?"

Somehow Leigh managed to put a coolness into her voice. "I don't think that's any of your business."

His smile was not a nice one. "That means there probably is. Does he know you're married?"

Abruptly Leigh pushed away from the window sill. She took a deep breath, reconsidered and decided to try once more.

"Jason, let's end the war. If we're going to be living together—I mean, sharing the same house—for the next few months, we've got to try to be civil at least. It isn't going to help Jody if we're constantly sniping at one another. Children must be sensitive to atmosphere."

She paused, searching the cold face in vain for an ounce of understanding.

"Just what did you have in mind?" he asked suggestively.

Helpless, Leigh whirled away from his derision. "Oh, what's the use? I'm going to bed."

She had reached the door of her room when he caught up with her.

"Leigh, wait." He caught her shoulder. "You're right. I'll bury the hatchet—for Jody's sake."

She stared at him open-mouthed, his capitulation taking her completely by surprise.

"*Pax?*"

Unnervingly conscious of his closeness, Leigh was suddenly breathless and could only nod. His hand inched up to trail light fingertips across her smooth cheek, his breath stirring a few strands of the silvery hair about her temple.

Before she was really aware of what he was doing, he leaned over and she felt his lips brush hers. They lingered as their kiss deepened. Her lips parted, and almost involuntarily, she swayed against him. "Good night, my love, sleep well," he said softly. He lifted his head, and for a magic instant, his dark eyes met hers. Then he moved away and went to his room, gently closing the door.

As in a daze, Leigh went into her bedroom. But once in bed, she found it hard to get to sleep. She tried to tell herself it was the unfamiliar bed, a strange house, her new responsibilities with Jody, but she had to be honest with herself. It was Jason. Her lips still tingled from their kiss. She had to admit that she was still as physically attracted to him as ever. Had he not stopped when he had, God knows where it all would have ended. Just to hear his even breathing next door sent her temperature soaring. When his dark eyes had looked into hers, she had trembled with desire. His rugged features had haunted her dreams for too long. She had longed for too many lonely years for his touch not to be moved by it now.

And yet she hated him. She must have been out of her mind to agree to end the warfare between them. "*Pax*," he had said. *Pax* indeed! Being friendly with Jason was like crawling in bed with a tiger. She winced at her own imagery. Yes, she must remember that. He had never loved her. He didn't now. Nothing had changed. That he still found her desirable was due to their proximity. She had always known, even in their few weeks together, that Jason was a passionate man, but passion is not love, she reminded herself.

She had offered him her heart five years ago with all the idealism of a first love, and he had carelessly accepted it. But he hadn't given her anything in return. Worse, she had a strong suspicion that he had spoiled her for any other man.

Hate him though she might, Leigh wasn't fool enough to underestimate his pure physical appeal. Therein lay her danger. She knew she had to guard against being drawn helplessly into the powerful magnetic field that surrounded him. She couldn't let that happen. She just couldn't.

Absently Leigh rubbed her hand across her forehead. She had to cope with the situation if she was to last out the next weeks, and the best way would seem to be to keep her mind off Jason.

Rolling over, Leigh punched her pillow up and determinedly closed her eyes.

Still, when Jody began to stir around six o'clock, she was glad of an excuse to get up.

Chapter Four

The next few days sped by. Leigh adjusted without difficulty to Jody's simple routine. The child was increasingly affectionate as she got used to Leigh and the two of them spent happy, full hours together. The warm spring weather cooperated so that they were able to spend most of their time out of doors. They rambled in the woods as far as Jody's short legs could go without tiring, and they explored the neighborhood. As Jason had said, the cottage was rather isolated so there were no near neighbors, but Jody seemed content with Leigh's company. She was an amenable child and since she was Leigh's primary concern, Leigh gave her all her attention. In doing so, she hoped she wasn't spoiling the child, but so far she saw no evidence of it, and she was learning to be firm when necessary.

Much to Leigh's relief, the situation between

Jason and her was easier than it had been. True to his word, he had buried the hatchet, for the time being anyway, for Jody's sake. Leigh couldn't penetrate the thoughts behind his enigmatic mask, but on the surface he was casual and relaxed with her. In fact, he had taken lately to treating her much the way he treated Jody, with gentle teasing.

They didn't see much of him, however. He left very early in the mornings, often before Leigh and Jody were up, which was early indeed, and would appear at night in time for dinner. He always reserved some time in his busy schedule for Jody, usually in the evening before she went to bed. Afterwards, pleading work, he would bring out his attaché case and spend the rest of the evening immersed in a stack of papers. Leigh took to going to bed early. Often she was pleasantly tired from the exercise of the day, but increasingly, she found she didn't want to sit in the same room with Jason. Leaning over a table, an intense look of concentration on his face as he read or wrote, Jason was too disturbing for her peace of mind. The aura of virile masculinity about him was pervasive, even when his thoughts were totally on another plane. Somehow it would reach out to Leigh from across the room, repeatedly drawing her eyes from the printed pages of the magazine or book in front of her. So, in self-defense, she took refuge in her room.

One morning, Leigh and Jody had visitors. Since the sky was rather overcast, Leigh had convinced Jody to pass up their usual walk in favor of an art project. She had found a stack of old magazines in a closet and she was cutting bright pictures from them for Jody to paste onto a large piece of paper. So engrossed were they that they didn't hear anyone knocking on the door and they looked up to see a woman and a little girl of five or so walking into the kitchen.

"Mrs. Randall?" The woman hesitated until Leigh nodded. "I did knock," she said, smiling. "When I saw the door was open, I knew you must be here so we came on in. I hope you don't mind." She led the child forward a step. "I'm Betty Pender, and this is my daughter Karen. We live here on the farm."

Leigh smiled in return as she gave her name. "I'm sorry we didn't hear you. We've gotten rather carried away, I'm afraid," she said, motioning toward the littered table.

She bent to the child to say hello and perform the introduction of Jody. In the presence of the older child, Jody seemed shy as well.

"Maybe Karen would like to help you paste," Leigh suggested gently as she retrieved the scissors she had been using and put them away on a high shelf. Leaving the children to their cautious observance of each other, she turned to her guest.

"Would you like some coffee?"

The woman accepted, and while Leigh was busy at the sink looked with interest around the shabby, but now spotlessly clean room.

"I hope you don't mind my dropping by like this," she said, sitting down in the kitchen chair Leigh indicated. "I wanted to give you time to settle in, but I was dying to meet you."

"I'm glad you came over," Leigh assured her

warmly. "I like company and I'm sure Jody will be delighted to have someone her own age to play with for a change."

She glanced at the two children, who still seemed wary with each other. Jody was pasting, with Karen an interested onlooker.

"I heard about Bob's accident," Betty said softly. "It was nice of you to give up your honeymoon to take care of Jody." Her voice was full of admiration and Leigh felt like a terrible fraud.

Deep in thought, she opened the refrigerator door to reach for a container of milk. She had wondered if Jason would try to keep her identity and presence at the cottage a secret since she was here only temporarily, but apparently he had not. Betty obviously knew who she was. That Jason's wife would be an object of curiosity around here, Leigh had no doubt.

Leigh gave the children each a glass of milk and a cookie, which seemed to help break the ice, and suggested that she and Betty go into the living room if the children wouldn't mind.

Betty Pender looked to be in her twenties—about Leigh's age, in fact. She was an open, friendly sort of person who chatted away, telling Leigh about herself. Her husband was Jason's farm manager. Apparently Jason's extensive business interests had grown so much that three years ago he had hired Jim Pender to take over the actual running of the farm. The Penders had come here from a city, Betty said, where Jim, country-bred, had hated every minute of his job as an accountant there.

"He saw Jason's ad in the newspaper, and

here we are," Betty explained with a slight shrug of her shoulders. "If Jim has his way, we'll be here forever. This farm is his idea of heaven."

Her personal narrative finished, Betty turned candidly to Leigh.

"You were certainly a surprise to us. We were bowled over when we heard that Jason had brought a bride back from Raleigh." Her wide mouth turned up in a grin. "Of course, Jason keeps his business to himself and he's never been one to waste any time."

Nodding, Leigh busied herself with the coffee-pot, offering Betty a refill. She was uncomfortable, feeling more than ever in a false position with this pleasant woman. Leigh hated the thought of deceiving anyone and yet, here she was, forced to act the part of Jason's new bride when in reality she was not much more than a baby-sitter, with the so-called marriage between her and Jason soon to be dissolved. What would Betty think when she discovered the truth?

"You were a fashion model?" Betty queried, and then shook her head ruefully. "I'm sorry. I must seem very nosy. This is such a small community that everyone knows all about everyone else. Sort of a local pastime. When someone new arrives, well, you can imagine the talk." She spread her hands expressively.

Leigh forced a laugh and tried to relax. "I understand, but I doubt if small communities have a monopoly on curiosity." She sat back in her chair. "Yes, I am, er, was a fashion model."

"It must have been exciting—parties, discos,

meeting celebrities." Betty's voice betrayed a trace of wistfulness.

"Oh, it wasn't as glamorous as all that," Leigh disclaimed honestly. "At least, not for me. I wasn't one of the swinging set." She wrinkled her small, straight nose. "As far as my photographic assignments went, I usually got the early morning ones, for some reason." She gave Betty a gamin grin, an engaging change from her normally cool expression. "I hate to disillusion you, but a model has to go to bed early so she won't look like a hag the next morning. She has to watch her weight. And I could tell you horror stories about posing for hours on a hot summer day wearing a fur coat."

At the expression on Betty's face, she relented. "Of course, it can be lots of fun. Especially the travel."

Absently winding a lock of silver hair around her finger, Leigh let her thoughts drift for a moment. On the whole she was satisfied with her job. It had its compensations and she wasn't really trained for anything else. But Leigh had never had any illusions about her success, or her looks, on which that success depended. She knew she was in demand now because the blond, Nordic type was in vogue. Tomorrow, fashion might decree dark, sultry looks. Realistically, Leigh accepted that her good bone structure made her highly photogenic, more so than more truly beautiful girls.

Her musing was suddenly interrupted by Jody, who ran into the room followed more sedately by Karen. Each held a rather soggy picture which was presented in turn to the two women. So lavish was their praise that the children decided to go back to the kitchen to make another creation.

Betty watched them go and then returned to their previous conversation.

"You must find the countryside around here a lot different from New York."

"Yes, it is different, but nicely so," Leigh answered spontaneously. "I like it here." She realized with a start that she wasn't saying that just for appearance sake or to be polite. She did like it here. It had a quiet beauty that strongly appealed to her and somehow she was more content now than she had been in a long time. They talked for a while longer until the children called them into the kitchen. There were two more works of art to show off. Exclaiming over the one that was solemnly presented to her, Leigh found a roll of tape and attached it in a place of prominence on the wall.

With a sparkle in her gray eyes, she told Betty, "I doubt if the tape will do this wall any harm, do you?"

Eyeing the peeling object, Betty mused, "I guess the remodeling on Jason's house will be finished soon. You must be anxious to move in."

Leigh laughed. "Believe it or not, I'm getting rather fond of this place."

"Of course, you are," Betty answered pertly. "Jason's here. When you're in love, you don't care where you live. I expect you and Jason spend most of your time in the bedroom anyway."

Disconcerted at such plain speaking, Leigh quickly said that she had been thinking of fixing the cottage up a bit.

Although the remark had been made merely to cover her embarrassment, Leigh continued to consider it long after Betty and Karen had left. Why not? She liked to keep busy. She could easily put a coat of paint on the living room walls while Jody was napping. She would check with Jason as soon as possible, she decided.

Her opportunity presented itself that evening.

Jason came to the dinner table straight from the shower, his thick black hair slightly damp and slicked back. He had apparently shaved as well, because when Leigh leaned over to place a bowl of mixed green salad on the table in front of him, she caught a whiff of tangy shaving lotion. A soft, short-sleeved shirt of navy blue stretched across his wide shoulders, the top few buttons undone to reveal the strong column of his throat.

He seemed to be in a better mood than usual and even complimented Leigh on the food. "This is delicious," he told her, after biting into a thick slice of the mushroom quiche that she had made that afternoon. "I can't remember you cooking before. Did Flora teach you?"

Before answering, Leigh reached over to help Jody with a brimming glass of milk, catching it just before the white liquid spilled over the sides.

"No, Flora didn't like me messing about in her kitchen. I taught myself after I went to New York. I didn't want to eat all my meals in restaurants, even if I could have afforded it, so I bought a cookbook and learned by the trial and error method." Her soft mouth lifted at the corners. "Mostly error."

Leigh told him that Betty Pender had come by.

"That was neighborly," he commented. "What did you think of her?"

"I liked her very much, Jason. She's nice. But . . ." Leigh's fork toyed with a piece of quiche.

"But what?"

"Well, I was a little uncomfortable with her. I don't like pretending to be something I'm not, and besides that, I wasn't sure I was supposed to be meeting the neighbors like any ordinary wife. Won't it be embarrassing for you when I leave in a few months?"

Jason's lips tightened at her words and she could tell that he was angry.

"That's not your concern, is it?" he answered her coldly and transferred his attention back to his plate.

They ate in silence after that, but Jason's good humor seemed to return by the end of the meal, helped by Jody's innocent jabbering. Considering it as good a time as any, Leigh broached her idea of painting the living room.

Impassively he heard her out, his eyes on her delicate, expressive features.

"It's all right with me as long as you don't neglect Jody. She's why you're here, not to interior decorate."

Leigh was not at all deflated by his dampening words. "When can I buy the paint?" she asked eagerly.

Jason said that he would take her and Jody to Harrellsville with him the next day.

"But I have work to do, so be ready to leave when I am," he warned before turning to ask Jody about the intriguing paste-picture hanging on the kitchen wall.

Determined not to keep Jason waiting, Leigh was up and about early the next morning. She dressed Jody in a pretty pink cotton frock and gave her a picture book to look at while she examined her own wardrobe. Some choice, she thought, surveying the two dresses hanging in the closet. The black dress was much too formal for a morning's shopping, so it would have to be the green again. Sighing, Leigh took it off the hanger and slipped it over her head. The dress was plain, but well cut and the soft jersey fabric clung attractively to her slender figure. She touched her mouth with pale pink lipstick, brushed her hair until it was smooth and shining and turned to see if Jody was ready for breakfast.

The little girl was excited and happy at the prospect of an outing, and she asked Leigh if she might be allowed to buy something for herself.

"Of course, darling," Leigh assured her with a wide smile. "Oh, wait." She picked up her handbag and rummaged around inside it for some coins. These she put into Jody's own tiny purse of yellow quilted cotton and pulled the drawstrings tight before hooking it onto the child's arm.

Jody chattered all the way into town, asking Jason a thousand questions and speculating about what she would purchase. The big, luxurious car ate up the miles and before much time had passed they were there.

Harrellsville was not a city like Raleigh, but

rather a large town. Jason dropped Leigh and Jody off at a hardware store and gave them instructions on how to walk to his office when they had finished their shopping.

Leigh wasn't sure what kind of paint to buy, but a clerk helped her. Accustomed now to New Yorkers' rapid speech, Leigh liked the man's slow drawl and his long pauses between phrases, as if he were thinking carefully about each word before he uttered it.

After selecting three gallons of cream-colored paint, a brush and roller, some sandpaper and a can of turpentine, Leigh asked the clerk if she might leave her purchases there until she could return later with the car. He smilingly assured her she could, so she extricated Jody from the stack of folders she had been playing with, straightened them into a neat pile once more, and off they went.

A few yards down the street, they came to a drugstore, and knowing that Jody was anxious to spend her nickles and dimes, Leigh ushered her inside. There Jody found a whole shelf full of items in her price range. With careful deliberation, she chose a tiny rubber baby doll in a wicker carriage, a string of orange plastic beads and a grape lollipop. Leigh, in order to be prepared for rainy days, bought some crayons, coloring books and water paints after she had helped Jody pay for her purchases.

According to Jason's directions, his building was several blocks away, down streets, Leigh found, that had character, where the old rubbed elbows with the new. She especially liked the red brick Victorian buildings they passed, with their elaborate false fronts that made them seem taller than they actually were.

Jody got tired before they reached their destination, so Leigh transferred the two small parcels to one hand and swung the child up on her hip until they reached a small park. There they bought lemonade and a bag of peanuts from a vendor and sat on an empty park bench to rest and feed the pigeons that hovered nearby. They didn't linger long, however, because Jason had made it plain that he was busy.

The address to which he had directed them proved to be an imposing modern structure of glass and brick that blended in well with its surroundings. Letters cut into the stone above the entryway proclaimed it to be the Randall Building. Leigh was slightly shocked. She had had no idea that Jason owned an entire building.

His office was on the top floor, the reception area a wide expanse of champagne-colored carpeting that stretched to a wall of glass. Somewhat intimidated by the grandeur, Jody crept behind Leigh while retaining a tight hold on her hand.

"May I help you?" inquired a cool voice.

A woman of exceptional beauty sat behind the desk, her jet black hair pulled severely back to reveal perfect features in a creamy magnolia complexion.

Leigh's hand went up to smooth her own hair, and then to brush at her dress. She knew she was rumpled from carrying Jody about.

"I'd like to see Mr. Randall, please."

The woman nodded and lifted a perfectly arched brow. "Did you have an appointment?"

"No, er . . ." Before Leigh could explain, the woman spotted Jody, who was peering around from behind Leigh.

"Why Jody, darling," she said, rising from her chair. The cool tones became a shade warmer. "What are you doing here?"

Suddenly the woman was looking directly at Leigh, her blue eyes narrowing. "You must be the new Mrs. Randall." She extended her hand. "I'm Paula Knight, Jason's secretary."

Leigh shook hands, painfully conscious of her own dishevelment under the scrutiny of this perfectly groomed woman.

"I'll tell Jason you're here. He's been overloaded this morning, so it may be a few minutes. Why don't you and Jody wait over there." She directed them to a grouping of black leather chairs at the side of the room and disappeared through heavy double doors.

Before Jody had time to bounce more than twice on the soft leather seat, the woman was back.

"Jason will be out as soon as he finishes a telephone call. In the meantime, may I get you some coffee?" she offered politely.

At Leigh's refusal, she hesitated a moment and then gracefully leaned against the arm of one of the chairs, carefully arranging the folds of her deep pink skirt.

"May I offer my, ah, congratulations, Mrs. Randall," she said in a careful way that had Leigh wondering if her slight breach of good manners had been deliberate, for she had congratulated Leigh rather than extending her good wishes.

"The wedding was rather sudden, wasn't it?"

Leigh took a deep breath. "No," she answered calmly. "Jason and I have known each other for quite some time."

"I see." Paula Knight was studying Leigh closely, assessing the direct look in her clear gray eyes, the sweet mouth, the seeming fragility of her slender figure.

"I hope I haven't kept you waiting too long," said Jason in a perfunctory, polite voice as he entered the room. He looked unfamiliarly formal in his dark, pinstriped suit.

Before Leigh could answer him, Paula had risen and placed a beautifully manicured hand on his arm.

"Did you get everything arranged with Mc-Curdy?"

He nodded briefly and once again directed his attention to Leigh and Jody.

"How would you two like me to take you out to lunch?" he asked.

Once again Paula intervened. "Jason, you have an appointment to see Mr. Stone at one o'clock," she dutifully pointed out.

"Call Howard and ask him if he can come at four instead. He won't mind. If there's a problem, put it off until tomorrow." Jason sounded irritated.

Her expression hardening slightly, Paula walked over to her desk and picked up the phone.

After Leigh and Jody had freshened up in the bathroom, they left the office for the hardware store to retrieve Leigh's packages. Then Jason headed the car toward the outskirts of town.

"We're going to one of my favorite spots," he told Leigh.

Before long he turned into a parking lot opposite a rambling wooden building that shone pristine white in the sunshine. A sign hanging from a post designated it The Coach and Four.

The building was obviously old, as was the tall boxwood hedge that surrounded it. Aware of Leigh's interested gaze, Jason related that in the eighteenth century it had been an inn, a stopover for tobacco planters on their way from their backcountry estates to the market in Raleigh.

"Local legend maintains that before and during the Revolutionary War it was a hotbed of rebel spies. Some famous battles were fought relatively near here, you know, the Battles of Alamance and Guilford Courthouse."

He got out of the car and walked with an easy stride around it to open the door for Leigh and Jody. Taking Leigh's arm in a firm grip and catching Jody by the hand, he guided them into the building.

"What do you think of it?"

"It's charming." Leigh looked around in wonder. She might have been transported back in time to the eighteenth century. Jason had drawn her into a room that had been used during coaching days as a parlor. The furniture grouped around the cavernous fireplace, he told her, was a replica of that used in colonial times. The gracefully curved sofa and chairs and delicate mahogany tables had been imported from Europe by the wealthy planters.

Across the hall, the public tavern had cruder

furnishings, rough homemade benches and trestle tables.

"Don't worry," Jason told Leigh as he escorted them to the large dining room down a narrow hall, "the food is twentieth century."

Despite Jason's words, Leigh noticed as she studied the menu that some attempts had been made to offer colonial fare. With mischief brightening her eyes, she told Jason she thought he should try the jugged hare and Indian pudding.

"No way. I'm a steak and potatoes man. But you go ahead. Do you know what Indian pudding is, by the way?" Assured that she did not, he told her that it was a mixture of corn meal and molasses.

In the end, Leigh decided to have a steak, too. When Jason gave their order to the long-gowned, mob-capped waitress, he added a bottle of wine, saying that it was not every day he could dine with two such lovely ladies.

Leigh was just dipping into her sweet potato pie, a concession to the colonial atmosphere, when Jason seemed to notice her dress for the first time. It was a warm spring day and the restaurant was not air-conditioned, conditions which had led Leigh unthinkingly to push up the long sleeves of her jersey dress.

"Isn't that dress too heavy for a day like this?" Jason was frowning at her.

Leigh put down her fork. "Yes, it probably is."

"Then why the devil are you wearing it?"

"Because it's all I have," she answered sweetly. "When I packed to come to Raleigh, I brought only a few things with me since I mistakenly thought I'd be there for just a few days. That was until you came into the picture, of course," she added tartly.

"Why didn't you say something?" Jason's scowl was bringing his black eyebrows together in a fierce line.

Holding on to her temper, Leigh answered, "I've been managing quite well at the cottage, and I intended to pick up a few things at the first opportunity." How like the arrogant Jason to bark at her like this over something that was none of his business anyway!

He shoved back his chair and picked up the check lying on the table.

"Come on. We're going shopping."

Chapter Five

With single-minded determination, Jason propelled Leigh through the doors of an exclusive-looking boutique, Jody trotting along between them.

In an effort to avoid what she knew would be a harrowing experience of shopping with Jason looking on, Leigh sought a way out.

"It's time for Jody's nap," she protested, pulling her arm out of his ironlike grip. "Couldn't we put this off until I can come into town at a more convenient time. There's really no rush."

"It isn't going to hurt Jody to miss one nap. You can just put her to bed early tonight," was the inexorable reply.

"All right, then." Leigh summoned a bright smile. "I'll pick up a few things and then Jody and I can walk along to your office. There's absolutely no need for you to wait. You'll be bored. Besides, I know how busy you are," she prodded sweetly.

"Who says I'll be bored?"

With great charm, Jason smiled at the tall, gray-haired woman who stood hovering at his elbow and introduced her to Leigh.

"Take your time, Leigh. Jody and I will wait over here."

Leigh turned to the discreet displays of dresses, but watched out of the corner of her eye as Jason and Jody sat down on fragile-looking Louis XIV chairs, obviously there for just such a purpose. Jody, who considered that she had waited long enough, eagerly dived into the bag clutched in her hand, pulled out the tiny doll and carriage, and settled down contentedly to play.

Leigh selected a pretty pastel cotton dress, several skirts with tops to match and a lightweight pair of slacks. As an afterthought, she added a pair of shorts. It could get fairly hot here in the spring, Leigh remembered, and she might as well be prepared.

The helpful clerk showed her into a good-sized dressing room equipped with a floor-to-ceiling mirror, and Leigh quickly tried on the things she had selected, not wanting to waste too much of Jason's time. She was just tying the belt of a denim wrap skirt around her slender waist when the clerk appeared, carrying two long dresses over her arm.

"Mr. Randall sent these," she said in an approving voice. "He felt they would suit you."

The woman carefully hung the dresses up, smoothing them out as she did so. "Mr. Randall asked if you would please come out when you have them on so that he can see how they look on you," she said as she turned to go.

Leigh was fuming. *Model these dresses, indeed.* Just what was Jason up to? He didn't care what she wore.

She had to admit, however, that the gowns were beautiful. She tried on the first one. Of the finest silk, it was a pure, frosty white, a color that interacted with Leigh's silver hair to create a dazzling effect. Leigh blinked at herself in the mirror as the soft silk caressed her skin. She had never thought to wear this color. In fact, she wore white only occasionally, and then a more creamy, eggshell color. The gown's softly gathered bodice had a halter neckline that dipped low in the back, almost to the tight waist, and an A-line skirt that fell in graceful folds to her feet.

Jason has good taste, I'll give him that, Leigh told herself as she walked across for his inspection. She stopped in front of him, and not even her professional model's detachment helped to quell her nervousness.

He observed her closely, his expression bland.

"You look more like an ice maiden than ever," was his only comment.

Leigh fingered the delicate fabric. "Jason, this is a gorgeous gown, but I can't really see that I would have an opportunity to wear it," she said hesitantly, not wanting him to think she did not like his choice.

"You never can tell. Be sure to pick out anything you need to go with it—shoes, whatever." His words were an order.

As Leigh turned to go, he caught her arm and

leaned forward. "I'm going to miss those tight jeans of yours," he whispered.

Embarrassed, Leigh pulled away and hurried back to the safety of the dressing room.

She put on the other gown, a cobwebby black lace affair with a peach satin underslip, and returned to the shop to find Jason wandering restlessly around a rack of swimwear. When he caught sight of Leigh in the sophisticated dress, he gave her the full blast of his piercing stare.

He nodded carelessly and handed her the wisps of material he had in his hand. "Try that on for me," he directed.

When Leigh held the scraps up by the strings attached to them, they took the shape of a bikini.

"Now, look here, Jason," she began, "I might agree to parade around in front of you in those dresses, but you can think again if you expect me to model this." She shook the offending objects at him.

"Just be a good girl, Leigh, and do as you're told."

She gasped at the patronizing words as the shimmer in her eyes fueled into a blaze.

"No. I do not need a swimsuit," she said firmly. If the saleswoman had not been standing a few feet away, she would take a punch at his arrogant face, Leigh told herself heatedly.

Jason was amused. "Then what do you plan to wear when the pool is finished, as it soon will be? I don't imagine that anything will keep Jody out of the water and it's your job to look after her."

"Well, then, I'd prefer to choose my own swimwear, if you don't mind," Leigh said haughtily, reaching out a hand toward the rack.

Her wrist was caught in a punishing grip.

"But I do mind," he returned smoothly. "Now go ahead or I'll come and put that suit on you myself."

Aware of the glint of determination in the night dark eyes, Leigh knew better than to push her luck. She did not doubt that he would do as he said. Without another word she returned to the dressing room.

The bikini was of the very scanty variety, the three lime green triangles that composed it just covering her. Leigh looked in the mirror and shuddered at the expanse of golden skin the slinky fabric exposed. She was tugging at the halter and wishing for a wrap when she heard Jason's mocking voice outside the door.

"Need any help?"

"No thank you," she said, attempting firmness.

The door opened and there he stood. His eyes measured her, lingering on the swell of her breasts and the curve of her softly rounded thigh. Leigh blushed all over at his prolonged scrutiny. It was as if he were touching her without reaching out a hand.

"Not bad," he said finally, breaking the electric silence between them.

"Of course," he drawled, "you're a little skinny for my taste." With a mocking grin, he turned to go.

"I've just about had it from you, Jason Randall!" She picked up the article that was nearest at hand, which turned out to be a blouse, and flung it at his retreating back. She'd like to toss everything in this room into that smug face! He was having a fine time at her expense.

He wasn't through with her yet.

When Leigh went over to the counter where the saleswoman was folding her purchases neatly into elegant maroon boxes, she found Jason there, his wallet open.

"I'll pay for my own clothes," she whispered. "I have enough money and I'd prefer not to accept anything from you."

He ignored her and counted out a pile of bills.

"Jason," she hissed, too aware of the interested saleswoman nearby, "I said I'm paying." She reached into the depths of her large handbag, but he forestalled her as he casually threw an arm across her shoulders to draw her a few feet away.

"I buy my wife's clothes, Leigh. Don't continue with this or you'll be very sorry." The words were a threat, menace clear in his low voice.

Leigh wrenched out of his hold. She didn't want to cause a scene but neither did she want him buying her anything.

With as much dignity as she could muster, she straightened her spine and conceded.

"All right, for now. But I'll give you a check when we get home."

"Home?" Jason gave her a curious look, then shrugged. "As you like."

After Jason dropped them off at the cottage, Leigh and Jody spent what was left of the afternoon coloring in the new book Leigh had bought. She judged a quiet activity to be a good idea since Jody had had an unusually full day.

They had an early light supper, and before Leigh bathed Jody and dressed her in pajamas, she changed into her own robe. Then they curled up together on the living room sofa while Leigh read the little girl's favorite story, "Sleeping Beauty." She had just ended with "And they lived happily ever after," when she saw Jason standing just inside the doorway. So engrossed had she been in reading that she hadn't heard him come in, nor had Jody.

He put his attaché case down and walked over to the child, whose eyes were heavy with sleep.

"Bedtime for you, little one," he said gently, picking her up.

"Want Auntie Leigh, too," Jody murmured, so Leigh went along. She was now a permanent member in Jody's bedtime ritual.

The good-nights completed, Leigh followed Jason from the bedroom, clutching at the folds of her amber silk robe.

"I, er, thought you said you'd be late tonight," she said distractedly, wondering how long it would be before Jody was sound asleep enough for her to go back for her clothes.

"I did expect to be, but I got away early." He dropped down on the sofa.

"Have you had dinner? I could go and fix you something." Ill at ease, Leigh realized she was babbling, her voice sounding unnatural to her own ears.

"I'll get something later."

His eyes had not left her face, and Leigh felt the awareness flare between them with the suddenness of a brush fire. Nervously she licked her lips.

"Well, in that case, I'll just go and . . ."

"Leigh," his voice slid across the room to her, soft and silky. "Come here."

He didn't move, didn't lift a finger, just sat and looked at her. Leigh was mesmerized, gazing back at him, and time seemed to slow, to stand still until nothing existed in that moment but the spell that held them.

Leigh had known this was coming. She hadn't known when or where, but she was sure, all the same. She had seen it in his eyes today in the dressing room at the boutique, the small flame of desire that burned deep in the brown depths of his eyes. Jason Randall wanted her, and what Jason Randall wanted, he took. And the way her pulse was leaping, Leigh wasn't sure she could deny him.

Without resistance she moved across the room toward him and let him pull her down beside him on the sofa.

When his firm lips met hers, all conscious thought fled and her reflexes took over. Very lightly his lips touched hers, then moved to the corner of her trembling mouth, teasing until her nerves were screaming. He kissed her eyelids, her flushed cheeks, the tender hollow at the base of her throat. Leigh put her hand to his chest, feeling the heavy thud of his heartbeats. Slowly she slid her hands up to encircle his neck and to tangle in his crisp black hair. Her touch seemed to enflame him. With a groan he gathered her closer, sensuously molding her body to his.

"Leigh, Leigh," he murmured into the fragrance of her silky tresses. "I've been waiting for this all day."

His kisses deepened as his tongue teased her lips apart and he tasted the sweetness of her mouth. She responded with everything in her being, holding nothing back, giving kiss for kiss, caress for caress. She was floating in another dimension, caught in a fierce desire she had never known. She wanted him to hold her forever, to press her closer, to touch her, to love her.

As if in tune with her pulsing feelings, Jason leaned back a fraction and looked into her cloudy gray eyes.

"Come to my room, little wife," he whispered, his voice husky with desire.

The words froze the bemused Leigh. She actually felt ice starting to form all over her body, and her mind was suddenly crystal clear. Wife. Yes, she was his wife. He had married her without love and that's how he would take her. With desire. But not with love.

Unaware of her tumultuous thoughts, Jason pulled her to her feet and brought her hard against his body to imprison her in the circle of his arms. His head came down and he took her breath away in a possessive, demanding kiss. In spite of her resolution, Leigh could feel herself sinking fast, her knees were weak, her traitorous senses were exploding, and all she wanted was to stay in his arms. Marshalling every ounce of strength she possessed, she said the only thing she could think of that would ensure her release.

"Is this the payment you want for the clothes you bought me today?" she gasped out in desperation.

His face went white, a muscle twitching in his

lean jaw. Leigh watched the desire drain slowly out of his eyes to be replaced with contempt. His hands tightened for an instant on her arms before he threw her from him, and then without a word he slammed out of the house.

Leigh crept off to bed, shaking, as miserable as she had ever been in her life. She had known for days that Jason still attracted her, but she had not acknowledged until tonight the incredible strength of that attraction. His mere touch melted her body, even while the cold voice of reason was speaking in her mind. All Jason had to do was come close and her carefully imposed restraints dissolved into thin air.

In the next few days, Jason treated her with a cold civility. It was as if she was someone he had hired to look after his niece and that's all she was to him. Not that he was at the cottage much. Although he still managed to spend some time each day with Jody, he deftly avoided Leigh. Where he spent his evenings she had no idea. Often, lying sleepless, she heard him come in during the early hours of the morning, only to leave again for work a few hours later. How he stood such a punishing pace, she did not know.

As for herself, she fought the strain she was under by keeping busy. She devised little projects for Jody, and when Jody was sleeping, found relief in the pure physical labor of sanding down the living room walls in readiness for painting.

One Sunday afternoon, Jason surprised her by suggesting that they all go over to the main house.

"The remodeling is getting near the finishing stages and I'm going to need your help in choosing color schemes and such." He gestured vaguely.

If this was any sort of olive branch, Leigh was going to grasp it, so she quickly agreed and went to get Jody ready.

At the house they found that Smitty was resting, and since Jason had a few business matters to deal with in his study, Leigh took Jody into the garden. Way at the back, they came upon a swing made from a car tire. It was hanging on a long, sturdy rope from the branch of an oak tree.

"This swing was my daddy's and Uncle Jason's," Jody said. Clearly it had been her destination all along. "Will you swing me, please?"

Leigh helped the child maneuver her legs through the hole in the center of the tire, and cautioning her to hold on tightly, gave her a small push. Leigh was pensive as she kept the momentum going. Jason's swing, she mused. Somehow she had never imagined Jason as a child. He was too much a man, too strong and virile. A smile touched her lips. He must have been a handful, a willful little boy with a mop of black hair and mischievous eyes. Realizing the direction her thoughts were taking, Leigh gave herself a mental shake. It was bad enough that the grown man dominated her thoughts, she could do without conjuring up an image of the younger version. With a sigh she gave Jody another push and was rewarded by a shriek of laughter.

Jason came out before Jody had tired of the swing, but once she saw her uncle, nothing would do but that he give her a ride around the garden on his shoulders.

As Leigh watched them, she felt a pain somewhere in the region of her heart. Jason was so good with the little girl. He would make a wonderful father. Suddenly, without warning, a thought struck Leigh. Jason must be planning to get married again. Why else would he be redoing the house, if not for a bride? He had agreed to the annulment readily enough.

Shaken, Leigh leaned back against the rough trunk of a tree. One thing was sure, she shouldn't be the one to help decorate the house for his next wife.

Before she could find a way to voice her objections, however, Jason had turned Jody over to Smitty, now in the kitchen preparing dinner, and bundled Leigh up the stairs.

The kitchen was the only room downstairs that had needed major modernization, he explained, and it was finished. The addition of a glassed-in sun-room facing the terrace and the new pool were almost so. Upstairs was where the work would now be concentrated, primarily the addition of a bathroom to each of the six bedrooms.

"We've tried to let in more light and add modern conveniences without sacrificing the character of the rooms," he told Leigh who was inspecting a high-ceilinged bedroom, complete with fireplace. "There is quite a lot of Victorian woodworking in some parts of the house that we've preserved."

Her face alight with interest, Leigh smiled at him. "You have a beautiful home, Jason," she said sincerely.

"I'd like you to pick out paint colors or wallpaper, let me know what furnishings need to be replaced, that sort of thing," he said after a moment. "Expense is no object."

"Did, ah, did the house actually need all this work? I mean, was remodeling structurally necessary?"

Jason cast her a studied glance. "No, the house is sound. I suppose you could call it a whim of mine." He put out a lean, brown hand to touch a wooden mantle shelf above the fireplace. "The time had come for a change of life style. I wanted to live more—comfortably, let's say."

He guided her into another room, done in shades of brown and mushroom beige.

Leigh looked around the spacious, airy bedroom that was filled with lustrous oak furniture. Moving from the large four-poster bed, she went to a love seat and several matching chairs grouped around an imposing fieldstone fireplace.

"Oh, how lovely," she exclaimed impulsively. "What a cozy spot to curl up and read."

"I take it you like my bedroom, Leigh." Jason's voice was dry as he joined her by the apricot velvet love seat. "Would you have enjoyed long, quiet evenings here beside the fire with me?"

Yes, yes, screamed Leigh's senses silently, his words creating a forbidden image. Jason, who stood suffocatingly near, stretched out his hand to tip her face up to his. Leigh couldn't have moved if someone yelled fire. It was all she could do to keep the sudden longing she felt from showing on her face, from being revealed to the keen, tormenting eyes watching her so closely.

In self-defense she stepped back, away from him, her wariness intensified.

She knew exactly what he was up to. He was playing with her, showing her what she could have had if she hadn't run away.

With as much composure as she could dredge up, she walked over to a door set into the wall at the side of the room.

"What's in here?"

Jason came and opened the door for her.

"The bathroom and beyond that, the dressing room. Both are going to be enlarged," he added indifferently.

He seemed to lose interest in the tour and motioned Leigh out.

Leigh led the way, but she was trembling inside, afraid of the cold purpose she had sensed in Jason, a man who could create a taunting moment of intimacy between them, deliberately, and then walk coolly away from it. She knew she had to keep her wits about her if she was to emerge unscathed from her relationship with Jason. If she could just keep in mind what he had done, how he had coldly and calculatedly picked her out to be his wife of convenience while letting her think he cared for her. She couldn't trust him an inch.

Downstairs, Leigh discovered that Smitty had cooked dinner for them, and gratefully offered to help. The taciturn Smitty allowed her to take the dishes from the kitchen into the dining room.

The house had been built in the days when large families were the rule, especially on farms where many sons and daughters were needed to help with the work, and the dining room reflected that past. It could comfortably seat twenty-five people, Leigh decided. Several leaves had been removed from the burnished mahogany table, which converted it from oval to round and made it more convenient for the four of them. Against one wall stood a lovely Hepplewhite sideboard, a collector's item, as were the matching chairs around the table. Someone had drawn the gold velvet curtains, shutting out the setting sun, and in the candlelight the room had an old-world charm.

Smitty was a superb cook. She pressed any number of fresh vegetables and the succulent prime rib, swimming in rich juices, on Leigh, who gave in and had an unaccustomed second helping. She almost regretted that extra portion, delectable though it had been, when Smitty served her a large wedge of homemade apple pie, but she managed to finish even that.

"Everything was delicious, Smitty," Leigh said, folding her napkin. "I'll bet I just gained five pounds."

"You could use it," the older woman returned. Leigh caught a flicker of amusement in Jason's eyes.

They took their coffee into the living room, Jody tagging happily along. It was quite a treat for her to be out this late.

Somehow they seemed to be regaining their old footing, for Jason was not as stiff with Leigh and the atmosphere between them was less strained. They were just arguing pleasantly over a book they had both recently read when they heard the front doorbell.

"Now who could that be?" Jason muttered, standing up.

Within minutes Smitty was showing Paula Knight into the room. Stunning in a scarlet jumpsuit, the woman went straight to Jason.

"I'm so sorry to burst in on you like this, Jason, but my car is acting up." As she paused she saw Leigh across the room.

"Oh, Mrs. Randall. I didn't realize you were here." The words hung lamely on the air.

"That's perfectly all right, Miss Knight." Leigh picked up the heavy silver coffeepot. "Will you have some coffee?"

"Thank you, no. I didn't mean to interrupt your evening, but," she turned wide blue eyes to Jason, "my car is making a funny noise and I didn't want to try to drive it home and chance breaking down. Since I was near here, I thought I'd call on Jason."

At the appeal in the blue eyes, Jason visibly softened. "Of course, Paula, that was the thing to do. I'll go take a look at it. Won't be a minute." He started toward the door.

Paula was right behind him. "I'd like to come with you if you don't mind. That way, I can get some idea of what the problem is."

When Smitty came in for the tray ten minutes later, she found Leigh staring vacantly at the carpet, her coffee cold in the cup.

"Are you going to let her get away with it?" she asked sharply.

"What?" Leigh looked up, startled.

"You know what I mean. The secretary. This isn't the first time she's dropped in here on one pretext or another." Smitty's hands went to perch on her narrow hips.

"She's been after Jason since before you came here, and it looks like not even a wife will stop her."

"I don't have any right to stop her, Smitty. You know that."

"Don't you?" With a disgusted snort, Smitty picked up the tray and went back to the kitchen.

After a few minutes, Jason returned to report that he couldn't find the trouble with the car, and since Paula was reluctant to drive it, he would take her home once he had dropped Leigh and Jody off at the cottage.

Leigh collected Jody, thanked Smitty for the meal, and followed Jason outside. During the short ride, she was very quiet. She had a lot to think about.

Chapter Six

One last swish with the small brush and Leigh was finished. It was a good thing there wasn't another strip of molding to do, she decided, peering into the now empty paint can.

Leigh had enjoyed herself. After she had brushed down the walls, she had rollered with enthusiasm, stepping back now and again to admire her handiwork. The once-mottled walls shone a gleaming white. It was surprising what a fresh coat of paint could do.

With a sigh of satisfaction, Leigh got to her feet. Oh, but she could use a hot bath once all this lot was cleared away, she told herself.

She gathered up the newspapers that lined the living room floor and bundled them under one arm. With the paint can and brush carefully balanced in the other hand, she made her precarious way to the kitchen. There she plopped everything disposable into the large garbage can and went to check on Jody.

The child was still sleeping soundly, her favorite stuffed bear cuddled under her arm. Leigh tiptoed out, closing the door quietly behind her. She hoped the barrier of the door would be sufficient to keep the paint fumes to a minimum. The clerk in the hardware store had assured her the paint was a quick-drying one, but still, a picnic supper outside this evening would probably be a good idea.

She was in the kitchen putting the brush in a pail of turpentine to soak when she heard a call from the open front door.

A thin blond man wearing a well-cut tan suit stood there, peering short-sightedly into the room as if trying to adjust his eyes from the brightness outside.

"Dan!" Leigh cried incredulously. "What in the world are you doing here?"

At the sound of her voice, relief showed in the boyishly attractive face. "I might ask you the same thing. Leigh, do you know what a time I've had tracking you down?"

He stepped forward to meet her halfway and take both her hands in his. At closer range, he gaped. "At least, I think it's Leigh. My word, what have you done to yourself, darling?"

Ruefully she touched the green bandanna concealing her hair and glanced down at the paint-spattered jeans. Not quite the way her agent was accustomed to seeing her. In fact, she doubted if Dan had ever seen her before with a hair out of place.

Leigh gave a helpless laugh. "I've been paint-ing."

"So I see, but I'm not sure I believe my eyes." He surveyed the room with its open windows and sheet-draped furniture, his nose wrinkling fastidiously at the strong chemical smell.

"What in God's name are you doing in this place? I thought you said you were going to Raleigh."

"I'm living here—temporarily, anyway. Didn't you get my telegram?"

"Yes, I got it." Dan's hands tightened as his pale blue eyes studied her.

"Are you all right? You were working long hours on that Lovelight ad just before you got word about your grandfather and I know how hard his death hit you. You had to get away, didn't you?"

His expression said she must have taken leave of her senses, but he was trying to understand.

"Dan, I . . ."

"No, not another word. There's no need for explanations. I'm here to look after you. What you need is to get back to New York, back to what's familiar."

To confirmed city-dweller Dan, life in the country would border on purgatory. He would never believe that anyone would willingly want to stay here. It was so quiet!

His arms went around Leigh in a gentle em-brace. "I'll take care of everything, my dear," he murmured into her ear as to a distraught child.

"Am I interrupting?" Jason stood in the door-way, a hint of implacability about his lean, hard form.

Leigh went stiff and Dan dropped his arms to turn around.

"Dan, this is my husband, Jason Randall." With an effort, Leigh introduced the two men.

"Husband!" Dan parroted. He was thunderstruck. Leigh, married! And to this formidable-looking man.

"Well, I can't say this isn't a surprise," he managed, extending a hand to Jason. Surprise was putting it mildly. Such impulsive behavior was something he would never have expected from the cool Leigh.

"It's a long story, Dan," Leigh was starting to explain when Jason broke in with the suggestion that they sit down. While he was taking the sheets off the sofa and chairs, Leigh went to the kitchen for cool drinks. From the looks of Dan he could use something stronger, but all she had was iced tea.

She returned to find the men seated and chatting amiably. Offering the drinks, she perched on the edge of a chair.

"I wish you the best, Leigh, you know that." Dan cleared his throat. "I guess I'll need some details. Do you, ah, plan to continue modeling now that you're married?"

"Why don't you join us for dinner this evening, Mr. Morgan. Then you and my wife will have ample opportunity to talk," Jason said easily. He leaned across to place his hand lightly, but possessively over Leigh's. "Are you staying in Harrellsville?"

On learning the name of Dan's hotel, Jason gave him directions to the main house, named a time, and within minutes they were seeing the agent to his car.

Leigh started to the kitchen to finish clearing away the painting debris, but Jason halted her.

"You didn't finish your iced tea," he pointed out, waiting politely for her to resume her seat.

As before, he sprawled on the sofa, but Leigh got the impression that the ease he conveyed was deceptive, that he was about as relaxed as a tiger, tightly coiled, ready to spring.

"Just who is he, Leigh?" Jason asked softly.

"I told you. Dan's my agent. He arranges my photo sessions, gets me commissions, sets up interviews, things like that."

Jason picked up his glass and drained it. "What else is he?"

"He's a friend. A good friend."

"How good?"

"Just what are you driving at, Jason?" Leigh was getting decidedly annoyed.

"Don't be naïve, my dear. I simply want to know if you sleep with him."

"That's none of your business," she spat out.

She had gone out with Dan a couple of times recently, and she liked him as well, perhaps better, than any other man she knew. He was kind and considerate, they had their work and friends in common, and he made her laugh. Also, he didn't turn into an octopus at the end of the evening. Just a good-night kiss at her door and he left.

"Answer me, blast it." Tired of waiting for an elaboration, Jason took Leigh's chin in an ungentle hold and forced her face up to his.

"I've been out with Dan a few times, but that's all," she capitulated. "I like him. *He's* a gentleman," she added with emphasis.

"Something I'm not, you mean?" Jason let her go and got up to wander over to the open window. "Did you ask him to come here?" he asked abruptly, swinging around and hooking his thumbs into the belt of his snug-fitting blue denim jeans.

"No." Leigh's eyes shot gray fire at him, her feelings stung at his continual distrust of her. "As I've told you innumerable times before, I'll stay until your brother and Clare come back. I gave you my word and I'll keep it."

"What about your marriage vows?" he asked strangely.

"What? I don't understand."

He chose to drop the subject. "Hmmm, I wonder what your good friend Dan wants."

Leigh took a deep breath, anxious for this curious inquisition to end. "He came to see if I was all right. He was worried about me."

"Maybe." Jason's tone was skeptical. In three pantherlike strides he was across the room, in front of Leigh. He took in her wide, misty-colored eyes, the perfectly formed mouth, features whose purity was outlined by the severity of the green scarf.

"Oh, he fancies you, all right. I could see that. But this is a long way to come for a fancy."

Jason raked an impatient hand through his coal black hair, leaving it in disarray. "We'll find out tonight, I suppose." He dismissed the subject of Dan and sat down again.

"Will you help Smitty with arrangements for the dinner?"

"Yes, of course. As soon as Jody wakes up, we can go over to the house." Leigh was relieved at the change of subject.

"You might as well plan to spend the night there. It will be too late to bring Jody back." He paused, rubbing at his chin.

"Maybe I should ask Paula to join us, to round out the numbers."

"I thought the idea was for Dan and me to talk."

"You'll have plenty of time with him, don't worry. If Paula comes, then I'll have someone to talk to as well." A sardonic smile edged his mouth.

"Then why not ask the Penders and make it a real dinner party?" Leigh challenged, only half serious.

"Why not." To her surprise, he nodded agreement. "You like Betty Pender, don't you?"

Leigh's affirmative answer was rather defensive. She was wondering if he was implying that she was immune to making friends or liking people.

As she went to rise from the chair, she felt a protest from muscles that had had too much unaccustomed exercise.

"What's wrong?" Immediately Jason was there to help her up.

"Nothing, I'm fine." She shrugged away from his disturbing touch.

"You overdid it today." It was a flat statement. He needed no other confirmation than the walls around him, which he was noticing all of a sudden.

"Do you like it? It looks better, don't you think?"

"Much better." But he was looking at her. "You know, Leigh, I didn't think you'd really do it." His eyes raked the slender form of the girl standing beside him. "You look too delicate to raise a window shade, much less paint an entire room all by yourself and still come out fighting."

"I'm stronger than I look."

"I'm beginning to realize that."

For one long, breathless moment he was gazing deep into her eyes, seeming to see through to her very soul.

At the familiar melting sensation that was flowing through her, Leigh broke the contact.

"I'd better check on Jody and put a few things into an overnight bag."

"Leigh," he stopped her with a curt command, "pack everything, we're moving. If we're going to have to smell paint, we might as well do so in comfort at the house." His smile was almost tender. "Who knows what else you might take it into that pretty head of yours to tackle if I leave you around here. My next tenant is already enough in your debt."

Her pulse rate doing double-time, she went to get their things ready. With Jason helping, the move to the main house was accomplished in record time. Basically they had only their clothes and Jody's toys to transfer, and the cottage to tidy and close up.

Since Smitty was not expecting them, Leigh

undertook to prepare their rooms while Smitty started on the impromptu dinner party. Leigh and Jody were given connecting rooms, and Leigh was glad the child would be near her, but it was a luxury to have a room to herself once again.

She stationed Jody at a small table with a box of building bricks, and humming to herself aired their rooms and put fresh linens on the beds. That finished, she went reluctantly along to do Jason's room, Jody trailing behind.

As she worked, she couldn't help wondering at Jason's change of heart in allowing her to stay in his home. Maybe he had tired of trying to punish her.

When she went to give Smitty a hand, Leigh found everything well under way. Between the two of them they were soon putting on the finishing touches, and Leigh even had time to take a restless Jody for a short walk in the garden before giving her her dinner.

Finally Leigh was able to have her long-awaited bath. She filled the lemon yellow tub with steaming hot water and sprinkled in a generous dose of the bath oil she discovered on the bathroom shelf. As she sank gratefully into the soft, scented water, she could feel the soreness easing out of her muscles and she stayed as long as she dared, giving herself up to pure, sensuous pleasure.

Leigh decided to wear the black lace dress. With the exquisitely groomed Paula Knight around, she would need every boost to her confidence she could get. Somehow the woman always made her feel at a disadvantage, but tonight would be an exception, Leigh decided, the sparkle of combat in her eyes.

With its high neckline and long sleeves, the black gown could have looked demure, but the skin-toned peach underslip peeping through the lace took care of that. The dress fit Leigh's slim form like a glove, the long skirt dropping in an arrow-straight line to her feet, and only a slit up one side allowed her enough room to take a step.

The gown enhanced the fragile quality about Leigh, its midnight color emphasizing her fairness. Despite the fact that she was rather tall for a woman, Leigh somehow conveyed a wistful, dreamlike beauty.

To accent the Victorian style of the gown, she swept her silvery hair into a knot at the top of her head, teasing a few tendrils out to curl around her ears and neck. Using all her model's skill, she brushed a silver-blue shadow onto her eyelids, touched her cheeks with rosy blusher and her lips with a matching deep pink, and she was quickly ready. She was just giving her makeup a last check in the mirror when the door to her room opened. Through the mirror she saw Jason appear, an elegant stranger in evening clothes.

"Closed doors are for knocking," she pointed out coolly, refusing to turn around.

"This is my house and you're my wife," he returned arrogantly, matching her tone.

At that, Leigh swung to face him. "Did you want something?"

He didn't answer, but his look was insinuating.

Leigh stood up, her carriage straight and full of unconscious pride.

"I'm ready, if that's what you came to see about." She walked over to the bed and picked up a black beaded evening purse lying there.

"What are you so nervous about?" he asked, too close for comfort, his observant eyes noting the slight tremor of the hand clutching the bag.

"Is it because I'm in here? Women's bedrooms are no novelty to me, Leigh."

"Well, I'm not used to having a man in mine."

He continued to stare at her a long moment before his mouth relaxed in a genuine smile, so appealing that it took her breath away.

"No, I don't think you are, little one," he said softly, so close to her his breath touched her forehead.

Discomfited, she was toying with the snap fastening of her purse when his next words brought her head up with a jerk.

"I've brought you a present."

He reached inside his blue velvet dinner jacket and brought out a small square case, which he handed to her.

"Open it," he ordered.

On a bed of black satin lay a pair of diamond earrings, the large round stones winking blue-white in the overhead light.

Leigh caught her breath with a gasp. "They're beautiful."

She closed the case and handed it back to him. "I can't accept them."

"Why not?" His voice was grim.

"They're too expensive, for one thing. For another, we're about to get an annulment to a marriage that never should have taken place. Why should you give me a gift?"

"Don't be so suspicious, Leigh," he said shortly. "I won't expect any—payment—if that's what's bothering you. The earrings are a trinket. I can well afford much more. The point is, to our guests tonight, you're my wife, and you'll look the part."

When she made no move to take the case from his hand, a muscle twitched at the side of his mouth.

"However much you may dislike me, Leigh, your soft heart won't let you make me the object of neighborhood gossip, will it? You'll look, and act, like a real wife tonight."

At his clever, absolutely correct reasoning, Leigh took the jewels and screwed them onto her earlobes. The glance she threw him was full of exasperation.

"You are an impossible man, Jason Randall. Does anyone ever get the better of you?"

"Not if I can help it. Although a certain beautiful blonde keeps trying."

As he started to laugh, she joined in, unable to help herself, and together they walked downstairs to await their guests.

Leigh wanted to check the dining room, to make sure everything was in place, so Jason equably accompanied her. The mahogany table was now extended to its full length, its burnished sheen highlighted by place settings of shimmering crystal and bone china. Instead of a tablecloth, Leigh had chosen to use forest green linen mats, whose color was reflected in the greenery of the centerpiece of yellow forsythia and buttercups that she had arranged in a round bronze vase.

Her inspection satisfactory, Leigh let Jason lead her off to the drawing room where he poured them each a drink and raised his glass to her. What his toast would have been Leigh never knew for at that moment Paula Knight walked in. Tonight the tall brunette was dramatic in an off-the-shoulder gown of translucent sea green. Leigh and Jason scarcely had time to greet her before the Penders and Dan arrived. Apparently they had driven up at the same time.

The evening went well. Smitty had outdone herself with the food, from the first course of finely ground liver pâté to the dessert of fresh strawberry mousse. Neither Leigh nor Jason had to strive to keep the conversation going, for it seemed that the others wanted to know all about Dan and his fascinating career in the world of magazine and television advertising. He answered their questions rather diffidently at first, but later, mellowed by the fine wine Jason served, he kept them amused with one anecdote after another. Although Leigh had been slightly nervous about hostessing her first dinner party, she realized that the good food and stimulating company made things easy. Jason helped, too, by replacing his usual mocking air for a relaxed, affectionate one. He was quiet, and every time Leigh looked down to the other end of the table where he sat, she caught his brooding eyes on her. She sensed a difference in him tonight, a change in manner that she could not quite pinpoint.

The Penders left soon after dinner was over, explaining that their baby-sitter had a curfew. From Betty's lively remarks and the smile on the face of her more laconic husband, Leigh could tell they had enjoyed themselves.

In the drawing room, Paula drifted over to Jason and began asking him questions concerning a business matter. Overhearing her, Dan turned to Leigh with a pensive look on his face.

"Your husband wouldn't be the Randall who owns International Trucking, by any chance?" he asked her.

"I don't know. I'm not really familiar with Jason's businesses."

Dan's lips pursed in a soundless whistle. "Unless I miss my guess, sweetie, you've caught yourself a big fish. If your Jason is who I think he is, he's a millionaire several times over."

Uncomfortable, Leigh picked up her liqueur glass and sipped at the almond-flavored drink it contained. Across the room, Jason and Paula seemed to be deep in conversation.

"Why don't we go out on the terrace," Leigh suggested to Dan. Now was as good a time as any to have that talk he had mentioned. He must be understandably puzzled about her supposedly sudden marriage and deserved some sort of assurance that she was planning to continue her career.

The night was warm and fragrant, the sweet smell of honeysuckle wafting on a light breeze. Leigh led the way over to a stone bench that overlooked the sweep of the lawn.

"Well, Leigh, you've certainly thrown me for a

loss," Dan said rather sadly. "I had hoped—oh, never mind."

"I'm sorry," she whispered. "Everything happened very quickly."

She intended to tell Dan the whole story, but she decided it would be better to wait until she was back in New York, with all of this behind her, if it ever could be. With Jason and Paula just inside, she could be interrupted at any time. And besides, it was better for Dan to get used to the idea that she was unavailable.

She had enjoyed going out with him, but she knew now that there was no chance for anything more serious than friendship to develop between them, and she didn't want to mislead him.

"I have a confession to make." Dan nervously pushed back the fair hair that flopped over his narrow forehead. "I was worried about you, but I had another reason for coming to find you."

As Leigh listened in silence, he told her about a commission he had secured for her, to model Alain Desmains's new fall collection in Paris for *Femme* magazine.

"It's a fantastic opportunity," he ended, his thin face alight with enthusiasm. "Desmains saw that evening wear spread you did for *Vogue* last winter and asked for you. Do you realize what that means, Leigh? He's the biggest designer in Europe. You'll be in demand, you'll have an international reputation."

She hated to quench his excitement but she had no choice.

"It sounds wonderful, but I can't get away right now, Dan."

"Surely you're not giving up your career, not now when you're right at the top. Your husband will understand."

"No, I'm not giving up my career, but as I told you, I need to take some time off."

"You're not pregnant?" He sounded horrified.

"No." She shrugged. "I don't suppose Desmains would be willing to wait a few months."

"Leigh, Desmains won't wait a few days. You have to go back with me now. He wants you in Paris by the twelfth."

As if to convince her, he leaned forward and peered at her in the half-light. "Every model I know would jump at this chance. You can't turn it down. Desmains would never hire you again."

Realizing that he was unable to shake her resolve, Dan lowered his head, a picture of quiet desperation.

"I gave my word, Leigh, that you would do it," he mumbled.

Even as she felt anger that Dan would make a commitment without asking her first, a surge of pity coursed through her. Dan was a nice guy in a tough, competitive profession. To get where he was today, he had had to hustle, and sometimes to make compromises with his ethics. Not fulfilling a promise he had made to the designer would be a serious blow for his credibility, she knew that.

Torn, Leigh wanted to help him out of a spot, but she was bound by her promise to Jason.

"I wish I could help," she told him, putting her hand on his arm.

"You won't change your mind?"

"I can't. I promised Jason not to work for—a while."

Their intense concentration was broken as the French window opened and Jason stepped out onto the terrace.

"Leigh, Paula is ready to leave. I was sure you'd want to say good-night to her."

Chapter Seven

"How about a nightcap?" Jason asked as soon as the heavy front door closed behind the departing Paula and Dan.

"I don't think so, thanks. It's late." It was late and Leigh was tired. She also had sense enough to question the wisdom of a *tête-à-tête* with Jason in the silent house.

But he wasn't taking no for an answer.

"Oh, come on. It's not that late. And besides, you deserve a moment to unwind. The evening was a success, thanks to you. You made a very gracious hostess."

"Thank you," Leigh said unsteadily. She was thrown slightly off guard, not so much by the compliment, but by the warmth with which it was expressed. In her momentary confusion, she let Jason take her elbow and guide her down the hall to his study, located to the right of the wide, curving staircase.

Without asking her preference, he went to the campaign table that served as a bar and poured her a small brandy. For himself, he splashed several fingers of whiskey into a wide glass and added a dash of soda. He took a long pull at the drink and then set the glass aside while he shrugged his wide, powerful shoulders out of his dinner jacket and loosened his tie. The formal white shirt he wore, with its tiny edging of lace down the front, looked almost incongruous on so masculine a man, Leigh thought as she watched him. And yet, the shirt emphasized his rugged appeal, its stark white a contrast to his deep tan, its fitted lines tapering closely to his narrow waist. He turned to pull the heavy curtains, seeming to enclose them together in the intimacy of the small room. With a casual wave of his hand, he motioned Leigh, still standing, to an armchair of burgundy leather.

She, however, shook her head, preferring instead to wander over to one of the bookcases. Somehow she felt she could keep her wits about her better if she remained on her feet.

The study was probably Leigh's favorite room in the entire house. With its book-lined walls and deep, comfortable chairs, it had an air of quiet and reserve that somehow comforted Leigh. It was a place to come to think, or a place to relax after the turmoil of the day. She could imagine Jason in here in the evenings, sifting through a mountain of papers, a frown of concentration between his dark brows. In some ways, the room, with its indefinable smell of old leather bindings and a lingering trace of wood-smoke from the fireplace, reminded Leigh of her grandfather's study.

Jason leaned back against the edge of the massive walnut desk, his arms crossed in front of him.

"Well, what did Morgan really want? I assume he came to take you back to the big city." Accents of mockery tinted the deep voice. "He seemed very persuasive from what I saw."

Too aware of his perceptiveness to try to hedge, Leigh went straight to the point. "He has a job for me in Paris on the twelfth." One arrogantly raised eyebrow forced her to continue hotly. "Which I turned down!"

He took note of her flushed cheeks and flashing eyes, a combination that heightened her usually rather glacial beauty. In one jerky movement, he tipped his glass and swallowed its contents, then crossed the room to the drinks table. With his back to her, he picked up a Georgian decanter.

"As it turns out, you could probably take that job." His voice carried the abrupt thrust of a rabbit punch to the abdomen.

He poured himself a refill and turned around.

"I had a letter from Clare today. Bob's leg is finally in a walking cast and his doctors think he should be able to travel in about a week. Of course he and Clare will fly here immediately once they've got the go-ahead. They're missing Jody."

The words registered slowly, and as they did sheer panic shot through Leigh. Not this soon!

She hadn't expected them to come back so soon. That meant she wouldn't be needed here anymore, that she would be free to go. In a week! Suddenly she was facing something she had known deep down for days, but had refused to admit to herself. Incredibly, she didn't want to leave. Not for Paris. Not for the Desmains's collection. Not for the greatest job in the world, or anything, or anybody. And the magnet drawing her was not this gracious old house or the lovely countryside or the happiness and contentment she had found here. It was Jason.

Leigh shivered as the chill of regret swept over her.

Jason's eyes rested sharply on her and she wondered if he could read her mind.

"You don't have to leave right away when Bob and Clare get here," he said almost reluctantly. "You're welcome to stay for a while."

"Thank you but I have a living to earn," Leigh got out. She wouldn't be the unwanted guest in his house no matter how grateful he was to her for looking after Jody.

"I'm sure you work very hard, Leigh. That's one thing I've learned about you in the past few weeks. But why not take a break? Surely you've earned it. Jody has kept you run off your feet."

Unable to trust her voice, she simply shook her head to indicate her refusal.

There was a long pause. For some reason, Leigh sensed an uncertainty about Jason, but decided she must be mistaken. Her own mixed-up emotions were sending her all the wrong signals. Uncertain was something the forceful Jason Randall had never been in his entire life.

With a click that sounded loud and final in the quiet room, he put his empty glass down on the table and moved over to stand behind his desk. From its blotter, he picked up a gold pen and idly twirled it, his attention seemingly focused on it.

"As a matter of fact, I'd like you to stay here permanently."

The strange invitation rocked Leigh. For a moment she couldn't move, and then realizing that she felt a little dizzy, managed to get herself into the chair she had spurned earlier. With fingers that shook, she carefully put the untasted brandy onto a nearby table.

"I, I'm not sure I understand," she stammered into the waiting silence.

He sat down behind the desk, looking for all the world like a business executive about to hammer out a complicated deal, and of course, that's exactly what he was doing, she realized as he spoke.

"I'm suggesting that we forget about the annulment, that we give our marriage another chance," he said crisply.

"Why?" Leigh croaked, for once deserted by her cool composure.

"Because I need a wife." He hesitated while his eyes ran over her, making the meaning of his next words very clear. "And I want you."

His dispassionate glance followed the emotions that chased across her sensitive features before he spoke again in a sure and convincing voice.

"It would work, Leigh. You seem to like it here, the place, the people." He held up a hand to ward off any interruption. "Don't try to deny it. I've watched you."

Leigh's fingers grasped at the smooth leather of the chair as she tried to come to terms with his suggestion. Now that the first shock was wearing off, she was beginning to collect her thoughts and her pride made her speak as coolly as he had.

"What makes you think I'd settle now for something I ran away from five years ago?" she asked, going right to the heart of the issue.

"We're both older and wiser, Leigh. More ready to accept that life isn't perfect. In other words, to accept reality." His face was impassive, his voice cool. He was making a plea for reason, not emotion. In fact, as far as he was concerned, Leigh realized, no emotion came into it. What he was saying was that they could have a working marriage if they put foolish dreams of romance behind them. Clearly he could. Jason Randall had never had any romantic dreams that Leigh knew of. But what about her? Was the starry-eyed teenager she had been when she married him gone forever? Would the adult Leigh accept a compromise?

She felt as if a lead weight had lodged itself in the center of her chest. Why was she even sitting here listening to him? Why didn't she get up and walk out and pack her bags? Was she so caught in his spell that she would actually consider this cold-blooded marriage he was proposing? She might want to stay here, she told herself, but not under those circumstances.

"You might miss your job and friends at first,

but I'd give you anything you wanted. I'm a rich man, Leigh."

"You make it sound like a business arrangement," she retorted, angry that he thought he could buy her.

He crossed his arms and leaned back to consider her soberly.

"It would be a real marriage, Leigh, make no mistake about that. I want a family someday."

Unable to look at him any longer, she dropped her eyes to the mellow red carpet at her feet. She should refuse here and now, but somehow, crazily, she was torn, tempted to say yes. She felt pulled in two directions and she couldn't seem to fight her way out of the maze of confusion that was overwhelming her.

She lifted her head and heard herself say, "I'd like to think about it."

"Take your time. You don't have to give me an answer right away. I won't press you." His teeth showed white in a lazy smile. "At least not until Bob and Clare get back."

With a shaky attempt at a smile in return, Leigh got to her feet.

"I'll go on up now, if you don't mind."

He stood politely and went to open the study door, and to her surprise accompanied her up the stairs to the door of her room. Half-turned to face him, she said good-night.

Jason's hands came out and took her shoulders in a firm hold. Slowly and deliberately he drew her to him, until her body was lightly touching his. For an instant he gazed into her wide, smoky gray eyes and then his lips were on hers in a hard, yet tender kiss. Leigh's very bones seemed to melt.

"I didn't promise not to try to influence you in my direction," he murmured seductively and let her go. "Sleep well."

Leigh hadn't expected to sleep at all, but she did. Her eyes closed fast the moment her head hit the pillow. What with one thing and another, it had been quite a day.

She awoke to sun in her face, streaming through a crack in the filmy blue curtains. As she raised her arms in a wide stretch, her eyes caught the sheen of the silk covering the walls, slightly faded now but once the delicate blue-green of a robin's egg. The room was still lovely, but it must have been absolutely gorgeous at one time, before the years took away some of its shine. Leigh was inexpressively glad that Jason had decided to redo it.

With a yawn, she swung out of bed, her feet sinking into the depths of an off-white Chinese carpet. It was then that the events of last night came rushing back to her. Leigh blinked and rubbed at her eyes, still misty from sleep. As unbelievable as it seemed in the clear light of morning, she had actually agreed to consider staying on here as Jason's wife. His wife! Had some mischievous demon taken possession of her?

Determinedly Leigh pushed the thoughts away and padded on bare feet over to the window that overlooked the vast back garden. If the view that met her eyes was anything to go by, the day promised to be a beautiful one, and suddenly she felt vibrantly alive and quite illogically happy.

She had scrubbed her face shining clean and was buttoning a sand-colored shirt over brown linen slacks when Jody bounced into the room. Her curls were tousled and her round cheeks were rosy from sleep. She must just have awakened.

"Hello, darling. You're an early bird today," Leigh greeted her. Hastily she clipped her hair back into a ponytail and decided to eschew makeup altogether. The fidgeting little girl was understandably eager to be out and about, so with a ready grin, Leigh swung her up into her arms and took her off to get dressed.

She had expected Jason to have breakfasted and gone, but there he sat at the dining room table, his plate pushed aside and the morning newspaper propped up in front of him. He was dressed for the office in a suit of a lightweight gray material, the blue silk tie he wore a perfect match for his shirt. Devastatingly attractive, he was the kind of companion a girl could spend a lifetime facing across the breakfast table, Leigh's errant thoughts whispered.

"Good morning." Her smile was almost shy, and he returned it with one of his own, wiped clear of mockery, that started the butterflies fluttering in Leigh's stomach. Telling herself she was acting like a teenager with her first crush, she hurriedly excused herself to offer Smitty some help.

In the kitchen the housekeeper, enveloped in a large, flowered apron, was dishing up two plates of golden scrambled eggs and sausages. These she handed to Leigh to take into the dining room, with instructions to come back for a rack of toast and Jody's milk, already poured and ready.

Leigh had put everything out and sat down just as Jason folded his paper and placed it beside his empty plate.

"I wanted to tell you that I'll be a little late tonight," he said, taking a last sip of coffee. "I should be back by about eight."

Leigh felt an odd pang of disappointment, but it was completely dispelled by his next words.

"Would you wait and have dinner with me?"

She nodded, and again with a sense of shyness, turned to help a clamoring Jody butter her toast.

"I'll see you tonight then," Jason said softly as he rose and came around to tweak Jody's nose. "Be a good girl today, pumpkin."

At the door he turned back as if something had just occurred to him.

"You drive, don't you, Leigh?"

"Yes," she answered, puzzled. "My grandfather taught me."

"Well, there's a car in the garage you can use. Get Smitty to give you directions if you plan to go far, though."

He tossed her a set of keys, and with a wave was gone.

Leigh decided to take Jason up on the offer of the car when she went into the kitchen with the empty dishes. A woman almost as wide as she was tall was there, in the act of depositing her purse and a large brown paper shopping bag onto a chair. Smitty introduced her as Carrie

Smith who came twice a week to help with the heavy work.

Depositing her bulk on another chair, Carrie accepted a steaming cup of coffee from Smitty and announced, with a hard look at Jody, that it was time she gave the floors a good scrub. Leigh took the hint and quickly invented an outing that would get Jody and her out of Carrie's way. A little questioning of Smitty and soon, armed with a hand-drawn map and a picnic basket, they headed for the garage.

They were in for a surprise. Leigh had expected the car Jason mentioned to be an old one, used for farm errands. Anything less like a farm vehicle than the sleek red Porsche parked there she had never seen.

Positive that there must be some mistake, Leigh took Jody by the hand and marched to the back door. She found Smitty in the utility room, knee-deep in laundry.

"Smitty, the only car in the garage is a red Porsche. That can't be the one Jason meant me to use. I'd be scared to drive anything so expensive."

"Then you'd better plan to stay home today. That's the one, all right. Arrived yesterday."

"You mean it's brand new!" In amazement, Leigh sagged against the doorframe.

"Yep. Jason said you'd need something to get around in, and he just couldn't imagine you in the pickup." With a chuckle, Smitty picked up an armful of towels and put them into the automatic washer.

Still reeling at the thought that Jason had

bought a car for her to use, Leigh led Jody back across the yard and they set off.

They had a glorious time. Following Smitty's suggestion, they drove to the northern end of the farm, to the site of a small pond used sometimes for irrigation and other times for fishing.

Spring was in full bloom. The belt of trees they had to walk through after parking the car was bursting with tender new green leaves. At the end of the wooded area, a lush meadow sloped down to the water which shone a clear blue in reflection of the cloudless sky. For a while, Leigh and Jody walked, after they had first put their picnic things down near the water's edge. They climbed the slight incline of the meadow where wild flowers grew in a profusion of vivid color. Once they saw a cardinal, its feathers scarlet tipped with black, hopping along a few yards in front of them. Intent on its prey of a fat worm, the bird didn't spot them, so Leigh put her fingers to her lips to alert Jody and they stood still and silent, holding their breaths until he flew away.

Jody liked the flowers even more than the birds. Every so often she would stop to pick a particularly pretty specimen. Leigh's favorites were the cool, wild violets, their delicate purple petals in such contrast to their dark green leaves. As they walked alongside a barbed wire fence, she saw a whole clump of the flowers just inside the enclosed area, and had to talk fast to convince Jody that it was not a good idea to climb under the fence to pick them. To the child's delight, while they stood there an inquisitive cow wandered up. She observed them placidly from velvet brown eyes, and then regally dismissed them in favor of a patch of sweet grass farther along.

After their ramble, Jody was content to rest for a brief time on the blanket Leigh had spread on the ground. Leigh sat beside her, with her arms loosely clasped around her knees, drinking in the beauty of the spot until the drone of a jet plane overhead interrupted her reverie. It was time for lunch anyway, so she unpacked the sandwiches she had made, the Thermos of lemonade and the fruit, and they ate their fill.

It was a very drowsy Jody she tucked into bed for a nap later at the house, the exercise and fresh air having taken their toll. Leigh felt much the same herself, as she told Smitty when she went downstairs.

"Whew! That child has more energy than a troop of Marines." Leigh grinned and dropped into a chair at the well-scrubbed kitchen table where Smitty was peeling potatoes for dinner. "It feels good to sit down." She glanced around the spotless kitchen. "Where's Carrie?"

"Her rheumatism usually starts acting up right after lunch."

Leigh could have sworn that the dour Smitty's lips actually twitched. Settling back, Leigh nodded toward the mound of tiny new potatoes and asked, "Can I help?"

Smitty lifted her gray-streaked head and for the first time since Leigh had walked into the room gave her her full attention.

"You look like you could use a cup of tea."

"Could I ever!" Leigh answered with a laugh.

In a fluid movement, she stood up and went to switch on the electric kettle. "I'll make it. Will you join me?"

"You won't want it served in the drawing room, then?" Smitty's tone was odd.

An incredulous Leigh turned around. "Goodness, no! Whatever for?" Surely she hadn't given Smitty the impression that she considered herself too good to drink tea in the kitchen.

"Miss Knight likes hers set out in the silver service and brought to the drawing room when she's here. She says that's the proper way." A brown curl of potato peel was plopped smartly down on the tabletop.

The singing of the kettle saved Leigh from having to answer, and before long, she had deftly produced two earthenware mugs filled with the strong brew.

Smitty shoved aside the potatoes to make room for hers while Leigh set out the sugar bowl and cream pitcher.

"So you had a good morning, did you?"

"Lovely. Jody did want to go wading in the pond, but I talked her out of it."

"The child's taken to you."

"She's a love." Leigh's smile faded for an instant. "I'm going to miss her."

"I guess Jason told you he's heard from Clare."

"Yes."

Smitty watched as Leigh absentmindedly stirred a third spoonful of sugar into her mug.

"Are you worried about leaving here?"

"Not exactly." Leigh picked up her mug, sipped and grimaced at the overly sweet taste.

"What's bothering you, then?"

At Smitty's tart question, Leigh jerked out of the abstraction that had held her. "I'm sorry, Smitty. I'm not very good company." She sighed and fiddled with a teaspoon. "You might as well know. Jason has asked me to stay," she said slowly.

"Well, you want to, don't you?" Smitty's shrewd eyes didn't miss much.

Pushing away the mug of too sweet tea, Leigh propped her elbows on the table and rested her head in her hands.

"Yes," she admitted. "I want to stay. But it's not that simple. Everything is the same as it was five years ago, except that this time I know exactly where I stand with Jason."

"Didn't you know before? He married you."

"Yes, he married me. He thought that if he had a wife, Bob wouldn't feel so guilty about leaving to take that job in South America. At least, that's what Clare told me when she came to my room after the wedding ceremony to help me change. I guess she felt sorry for me," Leigh said wearily. She saw no reason not to tell Smitty, who was, after all, part of the family.

"So that's why you ran off." Smitty shook her head as she got up to take the mugs to the sink. "I never knew. I didn't come to the wedding, you know, Leigh, because I was down with a bout of pleurisy." Turning to the cupboards, she reached up to a high shelf and took down a bowl, which she placed in front of Leigh, the gesture somehow conveying acceptance.

"Clare's all right, but she had no business butting in. Too meddlesome by half." With that

132

acerbic comment, she handed Leigh a small paring knife and shoved half the mound of potatoes toward her.

For a while they worked in silence, each busy with her own thoughts.

"Did Jason ever talk to you about his mother?" Smitty asked suddenly.

"No, he doesn't say much about his family. I do know that his mother died a few years before his father."

"She ran off with another man." Smitty said the words bluntly, her mouth pinched into a thin line.

"She never did like it here on the farm. Bryan, Jason's father, met and married her in Boston. She came from a socially prominent family, used to all sorts of parties, shopping, the like. I reckon the farm came as a real shock to her. It wasn't quite so prosperous in those days. The family had had a hard time during the Depression. Anyway, for a while, Jason's father pampered her, let things go here to take her places. But after the boys were born, he wanted to settle down. Not Marjorie. No sir. She got even more restless, started going off on her own, said she was visiting her family, but who knows what she did. Finally she just took off for good, with a man she met on one of her jaunts. Fair near to killed Jason's dad. He was crazy about her, and when she left he was never the same. He didn't care about anything after that, even his sons." Smitty's voice tapered sadly off.

"How old was Jason when she left?"

"Twelve. Old enough to feel it and to see what it did to his father. The boy took it hard. He had always looked up to his dad." Smitty sighed deeply, her light brown eyes moist. "That's when I came here, to look after them. Heaven knows they needed somebody. It broke your heart to see Jason. All the work around here fell on his shoulders and he had to grow up fast. He did, too. Got things in hand. Looked after his brother, sent him off for a good education." She paused, remembering. "Bob was younger, and it didn't affect him as much. And, you see, he had Jason." The last starkly spoken words carried a picture of caring responsibility and of loneliness for a boy too young to shoulder such burdens, and Leigh felt a lump rise in her throat.

Smitty's hands lay uncharacteristically idle for a moment. "So you see," she went on, "Jason's never had much cause to think highly of women." She sent Leigh a pointed look. "Oh, I'm not saying there weren't women in his life. The girls around here chased after him like mad and he's not a monk."

Embarrassed, she stood up, grumbling about wasting time and not getting her work done. She gathered up the now full bowls from the table and went to the sink.

"Thank you, Smitty," Leigh said softly. "I can understand much better now."

She did, Leigh thought, gazing blindly at the smooth surface of the table. Jason carried a scar, inflicted on him at a young and vulnerable age. And her own behavior must have reinforced it. When she ran away after the wedding, he must have felt that she was exactly like his mother, unable to stand life away from the bright lights. At least his affections hadn't been involved then, only his pride. Leigh wondered if the hurt he had suffered would ever heal. There was always the possibility that it wouldn't. But there could be a chance that patience and love could work a cure.

She shivered as she stood up. The question facing her was whether she had the courage to take that chance.

Leigh spent the rest of the afternoon with Jody, playing a game of toss in the garden with a big, brightly striped ball. After a while, when the workers had left, they wandered over to inspect the new swimming pool. It was kidney-shaped, set into a wide patio made of dark gray slate slabs. As Jason had said, the work was almost finished, just a few more turquoise tiles to cement from the looks of things. With Jody asking a hundred eager questions about when it would be filled with water, they turned to go.

Smitty had plans to attend a meeting of her women's club tonight, so she left a casserole bubbling in the oven. After giving Leigh last-minute instructions about its serving, she pinned on a beige straw hat and set off.

Unsure about the degree of formality Jason expected at dinner in his own home, Leigh changed into a simple cotton dress of pale blue. As she was brushing out her hair, she noticed vaguely that her exposure to the sun in the last few days had streaked it slightly, turning some of the strands almost white.

She went down and sat in the drawing room to wait for Jason since it was almost eight. On a side table lay a heavy tome which she picked up and leafed idly through. But then, feeling restless, she rose to go outside to stroll in the fast-gathering dusk. A slight distance down the driveway, she turned back to stare pensively at the gracious old home that had housed Jason's family for generations. Now, for all intents and purposes, he was alone there.

She walked slowly back, her thoughts centered on Jason. He was a strong, self-sufficient man, but Leigh wondered if he ever felt a need for someone to confide in, or just to be with. Despite his heavy business demands and occasional family responsibilities, he must be lonely at times. After all, he had no one person he could call solely his own.

He would have, if she agreed to stay with him. His request of last night had been simmering in her mind all day—while she chased Jody across the meadow, even as she talked to Smitty—but she had no answer. Leigh thought she could make him happy. She just wasn't sure she could endure the bittersweet pain that would come from living with a man who wanted her body, but not her love.

Chapter Eight

Lights swung in an arc around the driveway, illuminating Leigh where she stood by the steps. With the crunch of tires on gravel, Jason brought the luxurious car to a halt and got out.

"Were you waiting for me?" he asked as he walked over to Leigh, two bulky packages lodged in the crook of his arm. He looked very pleased when she met him halfway.

"A man could get used to this treatment," he said. Throwing a casual arm across her shoulders, he led her into the house. There, inside the hall, he handed her one of the packages, which was long and narrow and covered with green tissue paper.

The paper was unraveled to reveal a dozen long-stemmed American Beauty roses.

"Oh, how lovely," Leigh breathed. "Thank you, Jason." She tilted her face up to his with a mischievous smile. "A girl could get used to this treatment."

"That's the general idea," he said briefly, depositing the other package on a marble-topped table. He pointed to it as he turned toward the staircase.

"Would you put that on ice?" he asked, with a foot on the first stair tread. "I'm going up for a quick shower."

Smiling to herself, Leigh picked up the rather heavy parcel that was covered in brown paper and went into the kitchen to unwrap it.

A bottle of vintage champagne! Jason was really doing things right. Remembering that she had seen a silver bucket in the pantry, Leigh rummaged on the shelves until she found it. She filled the round container full of ice cubes from the freezer, twisted the magnum of wine into its depths and carried it into the dining room. After she had checked the casserole of beef and potatoes that was simmering in the oven, she got out a tall cut-glass vase and arranged the roses. About to deposit them in pride of place on the table, Leigh gently touched one of the scarlet buds, her mouth turned up in a dreamy smile.

"What a beautiful picture you make, Leigh," said a soft voice from the doorway.

Flustered at being caught in such an introspective mood, Leigh murmured something about making a salad and fled into the kitchen.

When she joined Jason in the drawing room a while later, he patted a cushion on the sofa where he had stretched out. Rather reluctantly Leigh sat down, too conscious of Jason's thigh only inches away from hers.

He had changed into black slacks and a matching black turtleneck sweater, the casual clothes molded to his strong physique. He looked supremely fit and altogether too disturbing for Leigh's peace of mind.

"Dinner's ready anytime you are," she said, nervously straightening her blue cotton skirt.

"Oh, are you cooking for us tonight? Where's Smitty?"

"Smitty made the dinner, but she went out to a club meeting."

"Then we're alone," he said, watching in amusement as Leigh attempted unobtrusively to shift a few inches away from him. A touch of his hand on her arm halted her.

"I looked in on Jody when I was upstairs. She's sleeping like a baby." Leigh chuckled at his small joke, and he leaned closer to trace the outline of her lips lightly with his thumb.

Fighting the bemusement that was swiftly stealing over her, Leigh gulped out a question.

"Did you have a nice day?" As the traces of teasing faded from Jason's face, she realized how tired he looked.

"We're having labor problems at one of the warehouses. A few troublemakers trying to stir things up." Absently he massaged the back of his neck with his hand, and Leigh had an insane desire to reach over and do it for him, to cradle his head in her hands and smooth away his fatigue.

"It will work out," he said, shrugging off her expression of concern. "Nothing to worry about. How was your day?" Clearly he did not want to go into the situation in more detail.

Respecting his reticence, Leigh plunged into an animated description of the delightful visit she and Jody had made to the north meadow, and as she talked, she noted that the lines of strain were easing out of his face.

"So you used the car? What did you think of it?" he asked slyly.

"It's a beauty. The nicest car I've ever driven." Leigh's answer came enthusiastically. "I wouldn't have thought, though, that a Porsche would make much of a farm vehicle," she teased.

"Sure it does," he said, his tone bland. "All that power under the hood makes it just the thing for heavy work, like hauling logs."

Was he suggesting that he had bought it for her use?

They went in to dinner. Leigh served the steaming casserole and the salad while Jason poured the bubbling wine.

"There's nothing like a quiet dinner at home," he said complacently, sounding, Leigh thought, for all the world as though they dined together like this every night.

It was an enchanting meal. The food was good, but the company was even better, Leigh had to admit. For once, all the tension between them had melted away and they laughed and talked easily, in harmony with each other. They argued over politics, but some of their ideas turned out to be incredibly similar. Jason had a stimulating mind and Leigh enjoyed exploring it.

But there was more than talk to the evening. The balance in their relationship had shifted, the undercurrents had gone largely because Jason's attitude had changed. Gone were the sarcasm and mockery. He teased Leigh, he talked seriously with her, and not once did he retreat to the old antagonism. As for Leigh, the hurts of the past were fading.

Their relationship was much more like it had been in the beginning when they first knew each other. There was a difference, however, and not such a subtle one. For Jason had treated the younger Leigh like a child, with a patronizing tenderness. Now he was treating her like a woman. Was he courting her? She felt confused.

However much she might warn herself that a friendlier atmosphere between Jason and her was insidious, she couldn't keep any barriers raised against his easy raillery and solicitous consideration. He crept under her guard and went to her head just like the sparkling wine they were drinking.

After dinner Jason helped with the clearing up, much to Leigh's surprise, and then they returned to the drawing room to listen to some music. Again he drew her down beside him on the sofa and curved her in the circle of his arm. Neither of them talked much, just relaxed and listened to the beautiful, rich strains of a Mozart sonata. Leigh felt Jason's body relax against hers and a sense of warmth and being needed rushed over her. It was a good feeling.

When the record ended, they continued to sit in peaceful silence until Jason spoke. "I have to fly to Nashville tomorrow on business." The announcement made a sudden inroad into Leigh's contentment. "I didn't want to go right now, but it couldn't be helped. I should be back by Friday."

Unable to get any words out, Leigh merely nodded.

Jason's hand captured a strand of her silvery hair. He coiled the silken tress around his finger and lifted it to his lips.

"What makes your hair smell so delicious?"

"I rinse it in lemon juice," she said, trying to keep a hold on sanity as her senses inevitably responded to Jason's nearness.

"I don't believe you, minx. It's more like roses and sunshine." His fingers rippled through the shining mass. "You're getting white streaks," he said, his eyes on the contrast between pale hair and cheeks flushed a soft pink. "You should wear a hat when you go out." Playfully he tickled Leigh's ear with the ends of one tress.

In retaliation, she reached over and tugged at the crisp black hair that fell over his forehead.

He made a sound under his breath and in the next second had pulled her to him. How could she resist? She went willingly, her arms curving around his neck, her mouth raised to his.

The kiss was a long exploration, deep and possessive and earthshaking. When Jason let her go, when she was no longer enmeshed in the heat of his embrace, Leigh felt as if a part of her had been torn away.

"This is getting to be a habit. A nice habit," Jason strove to lighten the atmosphere, but his eyes, their irises almost as black as the pupils, betrayed his passion.

"How would you feel about our getting away for the weekend?" he asked in a voice that was just a little ragged. "Smitty could look after Jody for a couple of days with no difficulty."

At Leigh's wide-eyed expression, he shook his head. "No strings attached, Leigh. I told you I'd wait for your answer. But it might help you to make up your mind if we see how we get along by ourselves for a few days. Get to know each other again."

Somehow Leigh found herself agreeing to go with him to a lodge in the foothills of the North Carolina mountains after he returned from Nashville.

As she undressed for bed later that night, she didn't kid herself that she wouldn't miss him.

For the next few days, however, she was very, very busy. Not only was she seeing to Jody and trying to help Smitty, but she found herself in the middle of the redecorating. The contractor whom Jason had hired to supervise the project came to see her and explained that the workers had reached the stage where some decisions had to be made. So after consulting with Smitty and not without reservations, Leigh pitched in. Jason had asked her to do it, she reasoned, and besides, she told herself with a slight tremor, this could be her home she was redecorating.

She selected paint colors and wallpapers until her head was swimming, and then poured over books of fabrics to choose curtains and upholstery materials. A woman was coming from Raleigh to measure the windows and furniture and make up the finished product. Once that was taken care of, Leigh had to drive into Harrellsville to pick out carpets and odds and ends from a department store which had a special service for projects such as this, the contractor told her.

When she was finished, Leigh felt a tremendous sense of satisfaction. She had done her best to restore the beauty and elegance of the old house, but she hadn't made it into a showpiece. One of the first things that had struck Leigh about Jason's home was the sense of comfort there, despite the number of furnishings that were collector's items. The comfort she had tried to preserve.

Leigh wasn't sure Jason would approve of all her choices, and she wished he had been there to consult, but the contractor had been insistent that the decisions had to be made right away or the work would stop, so she had bitten the bullet and gone ahead. Whatever Jason absolutely hated, Leigh decided, she could replace out of her own pocket. And anyway, she hadn't chosen anything wildly frilly and feminine, she grinned to herself. The one room about which Leigh was really unsure was the master bedroom. She hadn't actually changed much, but she had lightened the masculine beige and brown color scheme with touches of off-white and apricot.

"If he doesn't like it," the acerbic Smitty had commented when she saw the color swatches, "then he can just move to another room."

On Friday morning, Leigh broached the subject of her going away for the weekend to Jody. The child took it calmly, in her sober way, but Leigh feared that she might be upset. After all, Jody had been parted from her mother and father for quite a long time, and now if her Uncle

Jason and Aunt Leigh went away, that added up to a lot of separations for a three, almost four, year old to handle, Leigh reasoned. She talked it over with Smitty and then took Jody to visit Betty Pender and Karen in the hope that playing with another child would temporarily take her mind off the imminent separation and perhaps give her time to accept it. If not, Leigh decided firmly, they just wouldn't go.

The children had a riotous time on Karen's swing, while the grown-ups rested on lawn chairs nearby with glasses of iced Coke. On hearing about the proposed trip, Betty said she thought it was a terrific idea for Jason and Leigh to get away and immediately suggested that Leigh leave Jody there for the afternoon and she would bring her home later, in time to say good-bye to them. Then tomorrow, she said, she could take the girls on an outing. If they gave Jody something to look forward to, she might not mind so much that Leigh and Jason were away for a day or two.

Leigh could have hugged Betty for her consideration and went to talk it over with Jody, who nodded happily, her fat, brown curls dancing. To Jody, having a playmate for a whole afternoon was a decided treat, and two days in a row was miraculous. When Leigh left, it was with a much easier mind.

Back at the house, Leigh found Paula Knight comfortably settled in the drawing room, a tray of tea things in front of her.

"Oh, Mrs. Randall." She gave a self-conscious laugh. "Smitty said you'd gone out. I hope you don't mind my making myself at home." A be-ringed hand swept out in a graceful gesture.

Paula looked very businesslike today in a simple white blouse and slim black skirt, a scarf in a geometric print tied loosely at her neck.

Leigh wondered how the woman always managed to make her feel like an interloper. Besides that, Leigh's skin was damp from rushing about and her clothes were decidedly wilted. Yet, as much as she would like to go up and take a shower, Paula Knight was a guest and she was acting as hostess. With as good grace as possible, she sat down and smiled pleasantly. "Why don't you call me Leigh?" she suggested.

Paula acquiesced and returned the favor.

"I've been waiting for Jason," she explained as she sank back against the deep cushions of the sofa. "He said he'd be back late this afternoon."

"Is there an urgent problem?" Leigh asked in alarm, remembering Jason's mention of labor troubles.

"No, I have some papers for him to sign." Paula took a sip from the thin porcelain cup and looked at Leigh over its rim, assessing the simple skirt and blouse she wore.

"It's nice for us to have a chance to get acquainted," she said, taking charge of the conversation as if she really were at home. "I understand that you were a fashion model. It must be fascinating work. Do you plan to continue with it?"

Leigh was getting tired of that particular question, especially since she didn't know the answer. "I'm not sure," she said and asked Paula about herself before the woman could get in another query.

They made polite small talk, Paula revealing that she had worked for Jason for the past six months since his previous secretary had retired.

"He's such a dynamic man, so hard-driving," she shivered delicately, "that he can't help being a success. But of course you know all that."

With elaborate care she put the fragile cup and saucer down and leaned back again to pin Leigh with a curiously hard stare.

"Jason can be very ruthless." There was a brief pause. "In business, of course." Her glance fell to her nails, painted a dark crimson. She studied their oval perfection before she spoke again. "In his line of work, Jason often forms limited partnerships for a time, but when he's through with a relationship, he's through, even though the partner wants it to continue. Jason can walk away without a backward glance."

Once again the blue eyes lifted to Leigh, a message clear in their depths. Leigh felt she had been well and truly warned and she experienced an urgent desire to get out of the suddenly stifling room.

"Oh, really," she returned with some irony. "I don't know much about Jason's business matters."

"No, I don't suppose you do," Paula murmured. "I'm sure you couldn't have realized how very busy Jason is right now when you persuaded him to take you away for the weekend."

Leigh had had enough. She stood up, smoothing down her blue denim skirt.

"On the contrary, Paula, Jason persuaded me to go away this weekend, not the other way round. Not that it matters," she said softly. "Now if you'll excuse me, I'd like to let Smitty know that I'm back."

She made it to the door before Paula's voice stopped her.

"Oh, Leigh, would you ask Smitty to have some hot tea ready for Jason when he gets back. I'm sure he'll need something refreshing."

Suppressing a sigh of irritation, Leigh crossed the room and picked up the silver teapot, and then she made her escape.

Smitty was in the kitchen, noisily banging pots and pans and muttering under her breath. One look at her set face and Leigh decided not to mention Paula's request for fresh tea. She'd make it herself after she had smoothed Smitty's obviously ruffled feathers. She was sure she knew the cause. Paula Knight just rubbed Smitty the wrong way.

She made the tea and was discussing Betty Pender's suggestion about an outing for the children when she heard the front door open. Leigh arrived in the hall a few seconds after Paula, but Jason came straight to her and gave her a light kiss on the cheek.

"Hi. Did you miss me?" Not waiting for an answer, he put down his case and greeted Paula.

"Why are you here, Paula?" he continued with a slight frown. "Is anything wrong at the office?"

She came to stand close by his side, bringing with her a cloud of expensive perfume. "No, but

I have a number of letters ready to go out. I thought you'd want to sign them."

"This late on a Friday afternoon, it really doesn't matter," Jason said impatiently. "Monday morning would have done as well."

At the glimmer of hurt in the blue eyes, he softened. "Oh, all right. It was thoughtful of you to come all this way. Let's go in the study and I'll take a look at them."

While she waited, he turned back to Leigh. "All packed? Good. We'll leave as soon as I deal with this."

As Leigh watched the two of them disappear down the hall, Jason's head bent to catch something Paula was saying, she felt a sharp stab of jealousy. *Oh, no, you don't*, she told herself and marched determinedly up the stairs.

When she had packed for the weekend, Leigh hadn't been very clear on what to take. From Jason's brief description, she gathered that the lodge was of the luxurious, rather than rustic variety, so she put in a few formal outfits, but with casual things in predominance.

Her eyes on the clock, she quickly showered and changed into a matching skirt and blouse of blue-green silk. With a practiced hand, she smoothed on a colorless lip gloss and decided not to bother with any more makeup. She didn't really need it since exposure to the sun had given her a light tan.

At last, after good-byes to Smitty and Jody, they were on their way.

For the most part, Jason seemed to prefer to drive in silence, a brooding expression on his face. Several times Leigh tried to start a conversation, only to get monosyllabic replies in return, so she amiably shut up. Instead, she watched Jason sideways through her long lashes. He drove as he did everything else, expertly, with a minimum of effort and complete assurance as he wove in and out of traffic. His hard profile was etched with power. Intelligence, experience and confidence were there to be read in his face as well. Strain, too, Leigh's observant eyes noted, and she guessed that he had overworked. She was right, as he confirmed when they stopped for dinner.

"I only had about three hours sleep last night," he admitted finally in answer to her direct question. "I wanted to finish up and get back to you."

Flushing, Leigh bent her head and concentrated on her food for the rest of the meal.

"Do you want me to drive now?" she asked when they returned to the car from the roadside restaurant.

"No. It's only a little over an hour more."

Jason held the door for her and walked around to the other side of the car. After he had started the engine and maneuvered the sleek vehicle out onto the expressway, he seemed more disposed to talk. The meal had apparently refreshed him.

So Leigh told him how she had been working with the contractor for the past few days and described the various selections she had made.

"Sounds nice," he commented.

Hesitantly she admitted to adding some lighter colors to the master bedroom.

He quirked an amused eyebrow at her. "If you

like it, I'm sure I shall. Do you think it's attractive enough to tempt you to move in there?"

To Leigh's relief, he didn't seem to expect an answer but began to tell her about some of the places to visit near the lodge.

What with not getting away until very late afternoon and then stopping an hour for dinner, it was almost ten by the time they arrived at Blackstones.

From what Jason said, it had once been the mountain home of a tobacco baron who had spared no expense. The lodge took its name from the sooty gray, almost black stones with which it had been built. Leigh's eyes widened as she got out of the car at the porticoed entrance. Above her was a massive pile of stones that resembled a gothic, turreted castle.

"I wouldn't have believed it if I hadn't seen it with my own eyes!" she laughingly told Jason who was standing just behind her.

"Wait until you see the inside."

The tobacco baron, apparently seeking his European heritage, had put together his own baronial mansion. Jason told Leigh that on a vacation trip to England, the man had impulsively bought a stately home, parts of which he then had disassembled and shipped back to the United States to decorate his own summer home.

"It's fantastic," Leigh exclaimed, looking around in awe at the ancient tapestries that adorned the walls of the lobby.

While Jason checked them in, she wandered around, admiring the rich rugs, the burnished furniture, even laughing here and there at a particularly ornate piece. Finally the bellhop whisked away their bags and they were speeding up to the third floor on the elevator.

Jason stopped in front of a door. "This is your room," he told her as he unlocked the door and handed her the key. "Would you like to go back downstairs later for a drink?"

Leigh reached over and tilted Jason's wrist toward her to look at the thin circle of gold there.

"Uh-uh. It's late and you didn't get much sleep last night."

"OK, tyrant," he teased, his dark eyes warm with laughter and something else Leigh couldn't quite define.

"Shall I come in and tuck you in?"

When she smilingly shook her head, he sighed in mock despair. "Oh, well, if you should need me in the night, just whistle. Or better yet, knock on the wall."

He winked and turned to enter the room next door.

Chapter Nine

The telephone rang shrilly in Leigh's ears. She reached groggily out and succeeded in knocking the receiver off its rest. It clattered loudly against the tabletop and Leigh muttered to herself until she had grabbed it and lifted it to her ear.

"'Lo," she said, her voice slurred with sleep.

"Good morning, sleepyhead. Did you have pleasant dreams?"

Leigh's eyes focused on the face of her bedside traveling clock. "Jason," she groaned, "do you know what time it is?"

"Time to be up and out, sweetheart. We don't have a moment to lose."

Leigh rolled over, carrying the receiver with her. "Just another half hour. Please, Jason," she pleaded.

His chuckle came softly over the wire. "If you need any help getting dressed, I'll be right over."

Hastily Leigh threw back the covers. She didn't doubt him for a minute. "I'm up," she said, shivering in the cool early morning air. "Be with you in half an hour."

They had an enormous breakfast in one of the smaller dining rooms and then set off for a walk. Jason insisted that the view from one particular hill was superb, so Leigh good-naturedly agreed to the climb. Blackstones was located just where the aptly named Blue Ridge Mountains started their precipitous rise, and as they walked, Leigh and Jason could admire the hazy blue-gray peaks towering over them from the distance.

There were several pathways that led to the crown of the hill. Jason started along a well-trodden grassy trail that eventually left the trees behind to wind through a section of low scrub underbrush.

"You've been here before," Leigh noted, observing his familiarity with the area.

"A long time ago, when I was a kid." He looked down at her flat-heeled, strappy sandals. "Think you'll be all right in those shoes? The going is getting steeper now and can be pretty rough farther up."

A group of teenagers passed them, leaving the path to scramble up a rocky incline, with hilarious bursts of laughter at their slippery progress.

"Too hot for that kind of climbing," Jason remarked.

Leigh nodded agreement, but her mind wasn't

154

really on the boisterous group ahead of them. She couldn't help but wonder if Jason had enjoyed such careless fun when he came here as a youth, before family problems bore down on him, forcing him to grow up too fast. He was a serious man, but one with a good sense of humor, yet she just couldn't imagine him as an uninhibited, loud teenager.

As they walked, Jason's hand seemed automatically to find hers, his grip firm and sure. Leigh discovered that she liked holding on to him, striding along close beside him. They seemed in tune somehow, matched.

The day was slightly overcast, with a few heavy clouds scudding about overhead, but to Leigh, the colors were brighter, the air clearer, the pungent smell of the pine needles sharper than ever before.

They reached the top of the hill and paused to drink in the panorama before them. Although they had passed several people on the climb, no one was around at the moment and they had the place to themselves. The view was spectacular. Below, the vivid green of the rolling land met the blue-gray of the sky in a line delineated by a thin band of haze. They could see for miles, a seemingly infinite stretch of distant horizons, and behind them, the majesty of the mountains provided a stunning backdrop.

Leigh caught her breath. Her heart was beating erratically and she knew it wasn't entirely due to the view or the exertion of the climb. She was overwhelmingly conscious of the man by her side, especially so when his arm came around her shoulders and his head came down close to hers as he pointed out a landmark, a tiny log hut way down in the very pit of the valley.

Suddenly Leigh wanted to know—needed to know—what she meant to Jason. How did the two of them fit into this universe around them? Did he care for her at all or was she just another combination of flesh and bones to him?

She brushed away the strand of hair a fresh wind had blown in her face and tilted her head back to see him clearly. She did not pause to consider the wisdom of asking the question on her lips because if she did, she would never ask it.

"Jason," she said almost desperately, "if I decided not to stay with you, but to go back to New York, would you care? I mean, really care? Would it matter more than just in passing?"

Would the earth stop moving for you if I went, her heart was asking. Would you feel it, down so deep that the pain would be unendurable? Do you care at all?

Their eyes caught and held for brief seconds before his lids came down to conceal his thoughts from her. An enigmatic expression slid over his face.

"That's something you have to work out for yourself, Leigh, if you haven't already," he answered slowly, but with finality.

He took a step back, away from her, as if to cut off any physical contact between them.

"Don't ask me to help you make your decision. It's entirely up to you. I don't want to take the responsibility if you're going to get cold feet at the last minute. I want you, but only if you know

156

exactly what you're doing." The words were cold and harsh.

A tight iron band seemed to wrap itself around Leigh's heart. She stood and stared at him, her soft lips slightly parted in consternation. He was forcing her to make her decision in a void. He wasn't going to give anything of himself away. He had been hurt badly in the past, she knew, and apparently he wasn't going to take a chance now. Sadly, she faced the truth. If he could be so rational about it, then his feelings could not be involved.

Well, so be it, she told herself philosophically. What had she expected anyway? A strong declaration of undying love! Hah! Not from Jason Randall. Never in a million years!

With a lift of her chin, Leigh squared her shoulders. She wasn't giving up. She'd just have to work things out on her own.

Summoning a jaunty grin, she suggested to Jason that they try out the view from another spot, across the hilltop from where they now stood.

The journey down the hill was completed much more quickly than the trip up, and almost completely without conversation. They were each occupied with their own thoughts.

They had a splendid lunch, one that had Leigh vowing not to eat again all day. She just couldn't turn down the succulent smoke-cured ham, with its distinctive salty taste, or the golden yams, floating in a rich brown sugar sauce. However, she did virtuously draw the line at dessert.

The atmosphere between Jason and her had reverted back to easy teasing, due largely to

Leigh's efforts not to let the conversation on the hilltop get her down. Jason was rather quiet, but not forbiddingly so.

After so much food, they decided to spend the rest of the day lazing by the pool. Jason did halfheartedly suggest a game of tennis, from which Leigh prudently begged off until Sunday.

She went upstairs to rummage in her suitcase for the bikini Jason had bought her in Harrellsville. She pulled it distastefully out. As much as she would prefer not to appear in this skimpy excuse for a bathing suit, she had no choice since she had no other with her. With a shudder, she put it on, but studiously avoided looking in the mirror. She already knew that the amount of skin it exposed was a millimeter short of indecent, the slinky green fabric molding her softly rounded hips and swelling breasts. She tightened the minute straps that held the three triangles together and muttered a prayer that the thing wouldn't come apart in the water. Thank goodness for her terry cloth wrap. With her hair caught up in a topknot and her feet encased in sandals, she picked up a towel and made her way to the pool area.

She stood uncertainly at the entrance and looked around. The patio was not crowded. The overcast day had played its part in keeping guests away, Leigh guessed. Right now the sun had decided to shine, and in clear view, the heated pool was a dappled oval, the pure azure color that only the Mediterranean Sea can naturally aspire to. The water glittered and sparkled as the sun skimmed over it.

Spotting Jason stretched out on a redwood

lounger on the far side of the pool, she went across. In black swimming trunks, he emanated a strong aura of virile masculinity, not a spare ounce of flesh on his lean, hard body.

He lazily watched Leigh's approach, smiling in approval when she dropped her things onto the bright blue cushions of the lounger next to his and slipped off her wrap.

"You have a terrific body," he whispered, arching a brow at her.

Caught in the midst of kicking off her sandals, Leigh straightened slowly. "You're not so bad yourself," she answered coolly, sauntering off to the diving board. She executed a perfect half-gainer and surfaced to set off in a rapid crawl stroke for the opposite end of the pool. The heated water felt delicious, sliding over her skin like purest silk. She flipped over on her back and floated contentedly, counting the now fluffy white clouds above that looked like thick blobs of whipped cream in a bowl of blue. What bliss, she sighed. If one could only float as easily through life.

When Leigh reached the shallow end of the pool, she jackknifed around and headed back the way she had come. Suddenly the gentle cradle of the water turned hostile as strong arms grasped her around the middle and she was pulled under before she knew what was happening. She surfaced, spluttering, to find herself wrapped securely in Jason's viselike grip.

Ignoring her struggles, he pulled her head forward and put his mouth to hers while they slowly drifted, as if in slow motion, toward the bottom of the pool, until a push by his strong legs propelled them again to the top. Leigh realized that she had been so besotted by the kiss that she probably would have stayed on the bottom without his help, unable to think straight enough to move. Jason had that effect on her.

They swam together for a while in probably the most lighthearted time they had ever had together until tiredness caused Leigh to climb out. She made her way, dripping, over to the lounger and flopped down on its thick cushions to sit and admire Jason's expert thrust through the water, his arms lifting and falling in precise regularity in a symmetrical backstroke. Then, she adjusted the lounger to a flat position and rolled over on her stomach to let the warmth of the sun soak into her body. Within minutes she was fast asleep.

She woke to a cooling breeze blowing across her shoulders and a warm, tingly sensation down her spine. With a sigh of well-being, she snuggled further into the blue cushion and threw one arm above her head, until, more alert, she realized what was causing the delicious tingle. Someone was giving her a massage.

She rolled over and then wished she hadn't. Jason was sitting beside her on the edge of the lounger, very much at his ease, with a tube of suntan ointment in his hand. While she watched open-mouthed, he squeezed out a white curl and proceeded to smooth it thoroughly down her arms. Leigh's clear gray eyes widened in disbelief as the sensitive fingers moved on to her midriff and stomach, stroking her golden skin with a frankly sensuous touch.

"What do you think you're doing?" she hissed,

aware of the people who reclined on lounge chairs within hearing distance.

Nonchalantly squirting out another blob of the cream, Jason rubbed it onto her legs before he answered innocently. "Simply keeping that fair skin from burning." Leigh had not missed the quick rush of desire in his eyes.

"Er, thank you," she choked out. "But I think that's enough for now."

"Is it?" he asked, all too aware of the sensations he was provoking.

"Oh, definitely enough," Leigh said and she sat up. Her insides were churning and she was having trouble breathing. One touch of Jason's hands and all her longing was clamoring inside her, bursting to be released. And she knew what form that release would take, herself in his arms.

Leigh looked at the sky and stood up.

"It's getting late. I must have slept for quite a while." She turned back to Jason who had returned to his own lounger.

"I think I'll go in and wash off the chlorine." She brushed a hand nervously at her almost dry topknot and pulled on her wrap.

Jason accompanied her as far as the special elevator that was specifically for guests who used the pool and punched the up button.

"I'm going to have another swim," he said. "Why don't we meet in the bar at," he consulted his gold watch, "about eight. How's that?"

It was fine. It gave Leigh plenty of time, not only to have a long, leisurely soak in the tub and dress, but to get her wayward emotions under control.

The one outfit that was appropriate for evening that she had packed was the white gown, the one that Jason had said made her look like an ice maiden. Leigh certainly didn't feel like she was made of ice when she was around Jason. Certainly not ice. Flame was more likely. He touched her and she ignited. It was too bad she didn't have a red dress, she told herself humorously.

She smoothed the soft silk of the gown over her hips and turned around to peer across her shoulder into the mirror to see the back. The halter neck and low cut of the gown left most of her tanned shoulders bare. Aware that nights could get chilly here in the mountains, Leigh looked into her suitcase for the filmy square of white silk that matched the dress, just in case she needed a wrap.

In an effort to dispel the ice image, she used a bit more makeup than usual, a violet shadow to deepen the color of her eyes, a warm pink lip gloss for her mouth and added blusher for her cheeks. She had washed her hair that afternoon so she left it swinging in a smooth curtain of molten silver to her shoulders. Her hair had grown longer since she had been at the farm, Leigh noticed, giving it a last stroke with the brush.

She slipped on ridiculously high-heeled black sandals, also from the boutique in Harrellsville, and after a search, located her evening bag. It was with a feeling of confidence that she looked her best that Leigh sailed forth to meet Jason.

The cocktail lounge was discreetly lit, its interior a mixture of tables and chairs, low banquettes upholstered in red leather and tall stools at the bar, also cushioned in red. The room was fairly crowded, but it took Leigh only a moment to find Jason. To her eyes, he was easily the most distinguished-looking man there. She stood and gazed her fill at him before he saw her. The dark dinner jacket he wore fitted his lithe, lean form like a glove, and the formal white shirt showed off to best advantage a tan not acquired by sitting in an office.

He was seated at the bar, but at her approach, he slid off the stool and came over to meet her, his eyes widening in admiration at the sight of her.

"You've spent a profitable few hours, I see," he murmured, his intent regard not wavering.

"Do you approve?" She pirouetted slightly before him, a feeling of happiness at simply being with him welling up inside.

For an answer he took her elbow and guided her to a small round table at the side of the room. After he had given their order to the hovering waiter, he turned to her.

"I would never have thought that perfection could be improved on." he said in a voice that was warm and intimate and caressing. "You are very, very beautiful."

Leigh was speechless at the compliment.

He leaned closer to whisper into her ear, his breath warm and sensuous on her cheek.

"You do realize, don't you, that you've made it impossible for me to concentrate on my dinner." Small dark flames lit his eyes. "And they serve such good food here, too," he added.

Leigh sparkled with laughter. He was courting her again and she didn't possess the power to resist him.

The waiter appeared with their champagne cocktails in tall tulip-shaped glasses. Jason handed one to Leigh and they drank. They didn't talk, but sat, shoulder to shoulder, in silent accord.

Leigh glanced around the bar, which held mostly men, well-dressed and successful-looking, all carrying on busy conversations to the clink of ice in glasses. None of them could hold a candle to Jason, she thought, returning her gaze to his.

"What are you thinking about so seriously?" she asked him. She felt dizzy, euphoric. The wine must have gone to her head.

He smiled his special heart-stopping smile. "I was sitting here hoping that no one in this room can read minds because what I'm thinking about you right now definitely isn't for publication. Although from the envious looks I'm getting in return, every man here has similar designs on you."

With a gentle finger he touched a cheek that had turned a delicate pink and then signaled the waiter for two more drinks.

"Have there been many men in your life, Leigh?" he asked softly.

She shook her head. "No, not really. Just friends, nothing serious."

"Why? The men in New York City can't all be blind."

Leigh shifted uncomfortably in her chair and looked across the dimly lit room, now filling up even more as the dinner hour approached.

"I've been too busy working, I guess. Contrary to popular belief, all models don't run around till the early hours. Late nights and rich foods can play havoc with a girl's complexion and figure, to say nothing of schedules that don't allow much time for wild carousing."

"So your career is all important," he mused. "Is it? Does it fulfill all your desires?" The questions came at her pointblank.

"No, of course not." Leigh rubbed her moist palms together while the waiter set fresh cocktails before them. She didn't want this inquisition, but if they were going to let down their hair, she had a few questions of her own that she'd like answered.

"What about you?" she asked quickly before Jason had a chance to speak. "Is business your be-all and end-all?"

His eyes bored into hers, his look intense and probing. "I'd like a family to share it with some day, Leigh," he said bluntly, "like any normal, healthy man. I don't like living alone." The words rang out like a challenge, perhaps an indictment of her for denying him five years ago.

Leigh's glance dropped to the table, the old pain engulfing her.

"Jason," she faltered, "do you think we could ever forget the bitterness of the past and just be two people, oh, without old antagonisms that get in the way?" She kept her face averted until she was sure she could safely look at him without the longing showing plainly in her face.

"That is the question, isn't it," he said soberly. "Yes. I believe we can start over. That's what I want, Leigh."

After what seemed an eternity, he raised his glass to hers. "To our future," he said as the fluted goblets touched.

Heads turned when they crossed the dining room to their table, such a striking couple they made, the tall, dark man a perfect foil for the ethereal beauty of the slender blond girl. The ornate dining room was at the top of the hotel, and their table was by a long window that looked down on the valley below, where the lights of numberless houses competed with the stars that twinkled in the fallen dusk. When Leigh had drunk her fill of the scene, she turned to admire the beautifully set table. One long-stemmed yellow rose in a pewter vase sat in the center of the crisp white linen tablecloth, where shadows flickered in the glow of candlelight. The waiter handed her a large menu, but Leigh couldn't concentrate on the printed words and asked Jason to order for her.

A good decision, she found as she listened to him discuss the merits of various white wines with the wine steward before giving the menu his full attention.

"We'll start with *escargots bourguignons*," he ordered, flicking a warning to Leigh to protest if she had an aversion to snails. "A Caesar salad and the salmon soufflé," he continued.

When the waiter had gone, Jason told Leigh that the Caesar salad was a specialty at this particular restaurant, he had learned.

"As is the salmon. I think you'll like it."

She did. Shredded salmon enclosed in a shell of featherlight nutmeg-flavored soufflé topped with a cream sauce, it was delectable. Leigh hadn't realized that Jason was so knowledge-able about gourmet dishes, but then, there was a lot she didn't know about him. He was a complex, many-faceted man.

The evening was a memorable one, although Leigh knew that the food alone could not account for that. Jason could, however. They didn't talk much, or at least if they did, Leigh could never quite remember what they said. No words of love passed between them and no embraces. Yet, Jason made love to her as surely as if he had taken her in his arms in the crowded room. His hand touched hers where it lay on the table between them. His eyes caressed her face, and his voice was low and seductive when he leaned close to whisper in her ear. Leigh was happier than she had dreamed possible, her cheeks tinted a wild rose, her eyes a cloudy mauve, and she no longer bothered to hide what she felt from Jason. He had given her a special evening that she would remember all her life.

For her decision was made. It was not consciously arrived at, she realized, but a culmination of all the things she had learned about Jason and about herself in the past few weeks. She loved him. It wasn't just a strong physical attraction as she had thought at first. Jason was a man she would walk over broken glass for. The past had ceased to matter. He wanted her and that was all she needed to know. Her doubts had vanished in the wave of pure love that swept over her. He needed her and whatever he asked, she would willingly give. The pleasure of giving would be enough. That he had asked her, without love on his part, to resume the marriage, she now had the strength to deal with. And she would make him happy, or perish in the attempt, she told herself. Oh, she didn't kid herself that it would be easy. Jason was a demanding, overbearing, sometimes ruthless man, and she would have to bear the brunt of it. But he could be tender, too, and she would teach him to be loving. He felt something for her, and even if it was only desire, it could grow. As he had said, they could make it work.

After dinner, Leigh floated out into the hotel grounds in a haze, her spinning head not all the result of the light Mosel wine she had drunk. In the sweetly scented darkness, she walked close to Jason, her arm around his waist. When they stopped at the far end of the garden, she went up on tiptoe to kiss him on the lips. She wasn't fighting her feelings anymore.

Very gently Jason held her away from him.

"Too much wine, I think," he said in amusement. He bent to plant a kiss on the tip of her nose and then he propelled her back toward the hotel.

Leigh stopped him with a sound of protest.

"Jason, it's not the wine." She wanted him to realize that she knew exactly what she was doing. This was no spur-of-the-moment, wined-and-dined feeling. It was real.

"Let's go upstairs," she breathed.

After subjecting her to a searching scrutiny, he agreed. He seemed to sense that she was in earnest.

In the hall, he took her key and unlocked the door.

She took the key back without looking at it, her

gaze concentrated on Jason and the question in his eyes.

"Will you come in? I want to talk to you."

There was no need to delay telling him that she was ready to be his wife in deed as well as on paper. She had made up her mind, for better or worse.

He pushed open the door and allowed her to proceed him into the room.

Inside, Leigh stopped short, causing Jason to bump into her.

In the armchair sat Dan Morgan, a magazine on his lap, his shirt casually undone, his coat and tie thrown across the bed.

He rose to greet her. "Hi, Leigh, I got here as soon as I could."

Chapter Ten

In total confusion, Leigh put her hand out to Jason, behind her, for support.

"I seem to be in the way here," he said tightly. He took Leigh's hand from where it lay on his arm and dropped it, as if he were brushing away a bothersome insect. "If you'll excuse me."

Leigh had been frozen into immobility at the sight of Dan in her bedroom, but the click of the door behind Jason's departing back jolted her to awareness.

"Jason!" With a cry, she ran after him. He wasn't in sight, and she got no answer to a knock on the door of the next room, so she hurried down the hall to the elevator. By the indicator above the bronze doors, she saw that the car was at the main lobby level, probably where it had just carried Jason. Leigh wanted to bang on the wall in frustration.

Defeated, she walked slowly back to her room to confront Dan, who was standing in the open doorway, waiting for her.

"How did you get in?" she asked at once.

"The desk clerk opened the door for me." He reddened. "I told him I was a relative and had news for you." He looked at her set, pale face. "I didn't mean to cause trouble, Leigh. I did try to call first from downstairs. Even had you paged."

That must have been while she was strolling with Jason in the garden in such a state of euphoria, Leigh realized numbly.

"What are you doing here?" Mechanically she closed the door and moved into the room.

"Leigh, I had to see you immediately. I've got fantastic news!" In his excitement, Dan grabbed her hand. "I've been in New York conferring with Desmains and he's agreed to wait two weeks for you. Imagine, the great man himself, waiting for a model!"

Ignoring her complete lack of response, he went on, but more slowly. "At first, he was furious that you turned him down. But I talked him around, Leigh."

She couldn't have cared less. At the moment she would gladly have banished both Desmains and Dan Morgan to the Sahara.

She shook off Dan's hand and walked over to the center of the room, pulling herself together.

"I thought I told you I would get in touch with you when I was ready to go back to work," she said coldly.

"I know, Leigh." He had the grace to look abashed, but then the exultance came to the fore again. "But, Desmains . . ."

171

"I'm afraid I don't particularly care about Monsieur Desmains, Dan," she cut him off. "I'm just not available."

"What!" Dan was clearly astounded. "You'll be finished in the business if you . . ."

"Then I'll just have to sell shoelaces, won't I?" she said. "Right now it doesn't seem important." Leigh didn't think she could take much more of Dan or his persuasive tactics.

"I'm developing a headache," she said, realizing it was true. "Would you mind leaving, Dan?"

The expression on his face hovered between petulance and defeat, but Leigh steeled herself against feeling sorry for him. He had deliberately disregarded her wishes and gone ahead with this venture. The trouble he might now reap he had brought on himself. If only he had called her first, to check with her, he could have been spared all this. *They all could have been spared,* she amended.

Dejectedly, he picked up his jacket and tie. "You won't change your mind?"

"No," she said and then she softened. In spite of everything, Dan had been a good agent and a good friend. She went and stood beside him. "I can't," she said softly. "I have a marriage to set right."

Finally he took her at her word. "I shouldn't have barged in like this." Self-pity tinged his voice. "I've got a car waiting, so I'll be on my way. See you around sometime."

She walked him to the door, but halted him with a question as a thought occurred to her. "How did you know where we were, Dan?"

"I went to the house. Your housekeeper said you were away for the weekend, but wouldn't divulge where, so I called Jason's office and his secretary told me."

She would, thought Leigh bitterly, seeing Dan off.

As soon as she was alone, she went straight to the phone and dialed Jason's room. There was no answer. Impatiently she paced the floor. Where was he? She had to talk to him, to straighten this out. Undoubtedly he believed that she had asked Dan to come here, that she had decided to go back to work.

Again she tried his room, but still no answer, only the continuing buzz of the ring. Answer it, she begged.

Gulping back a sob, she picked up the filmy white stole she had dropped when she and Jason came into the room to find Dan there, and draped it around her shoulders.

If Jason wouldn't come back to his room, then she would go and find him. Switching out the light, she closed the door and walked determinedly down the hall.

At the entrance to the bar-lounge, she hesitated to peer through the smoky haze. At this hour it was less crowded than it had been earlier, and she had no trouble locating Jason. He was seated at the long polished wood bar, a drink in front of him.

He watched her approach, but when she reached him, he deliberately turned away.

"Hey, bartender, bring me another." The empty glass was hoisted. "Make it a double this time."

173

After he had a refill, he turned back to the waiting Leigh, running his eyes over her in an insolent appraisal.

"Well now, honey, what can I do for you?" he asked suggestively while an interested onlooker on the next bar stool guffawed.

"Maybe she's offering what she can do for you, buddy," the man chortled, eyeing Leigh himself. "Hey, little lady, if he doesn't treat you right, you come on over here."

Her cheeks burning in humiliation, Leigh touched Jason's arm in mute appeal.

"Jason, please. I've got to talk to you."

He pointedly moved his arm to pick up his glass and her hand fell away.

"Go ahead," he invited, downing half the whiskey in a gulp.

"Not here. Jason, I need to talk to you."

"This is as good a place as any. We're all friends here." He nodded toward his neighbor. "Right, mate?"

Then, as if he were forced, he looked at Leigh. "Well, what's on your mind?"

There was nothing but resignation in his tone, and he made no move to offer her the courtesy of either a drink or a seat. So she stood there, pressing her palms together and trying not to tremble.

"I didn't ask Dan to come here, Jason," she said.

"Oh?"

"No. The desk clerk let him into my room."

"How cozy for you both," he sneered, his eyes on the cubes of ice melting in his glass.

Biting her lip, Leigh leaned against the empty

bar stool behind her, its chrome edge digging into the small of her back.

Was there no way to reach him? she asked herself in desperation. This was not the time or the place, but she would have to tell him of her decision to stay with him. Surely then he would try to understand.

"Jason, I, I wanted to tell you tonight—I've made up my mind about the annulment," she stuttered. "I mean . . ."

As she struggled to find the right words, Jason swung around to summon the bartender with a lift of his finger. When he once again faced Leigh, he wore a look of utter boredom.

"Spare me the details," he said curtly. "I find I'm not interested."

Stunned, Leigh was unable to believe his words. It was a misunderstanding. He had to hear her out.

"Jason, listen . . ."

As swiftly as a jungle cat he moved, his hands shooting out to grasp her upper arms in a tight, bruising hold that bit into her tender flesh like knives. "No, you listen," he snarled, shaking her mercilessly. His eyes were blistering with fury, his mouth thinned to a cruel line. "If you don't get out of my sight right now, I'll do something we'll both regret in the morning."

In total rejection, he cast her away from him and she would have fallen if she hadn't caught onto the side of the revolving bar stool.

She straightened and faced him, a terrible look of pain in eyes that were brimming with tears.

"Go away, Leigh," he rasped wearily. "Go back to your boyfriend. Get lost."

Somehow she got herself out of the bar and up to her room. Through the hurt, she tried to think clearly. Jason was angry, perhaps understandably so, at finding Dan in her room. If only he would let her explain. She might be a fool, but she had to try, if there was to be any chance at all for them. Surely she hadn't rediscovered her love only to lose him again. Maybe in the morning, when Jason had cooled off, they could talk.

But in the morning, Jason was gone.

Leigh hadn't slept well, and consequently she was up early. Her first thought was to call Jason, but she wouldn't let herself pick up the phone until she got washed and dressed. If Jason agreed to see her right away, she intended to be ready.

She shook the creases out of her brown linen slacks and pulled them hastily on. With the pants, she teamed a skinny-ribbed summer sweater of cream silk knit. A quick brush at her hair and she went to sit on the bed while she telephoned.

No answer.

That's strange, she mused. It was very early for Jason to be already up and out. Maybe he had gone for a walk or a newspaper.

To pass the time, she tidied her things, neatly folding the dress and slip she had left lying on a chair last night and packing them in her case. She assumed they would leave late this afternoon since Jason had said he had to be back at work tomorrow. It wouldn't hurt to get a jump on her packing. She needed to keep busy anyway so she wouldn't have too much time to think.

The hands of the clock crawled slowly around until finally Leigh judged that enough time had passed for Jason to have returned from wherever he had gone, and she tried again. Still no answer.

I'm not having much luck with this phone, Leigh told herself in an attempt at humor.

Like last night, she'd just have to go looking for Jason, but hopefully, with a better result this time, Leigh told herself as she picked up her shoulder bag.

When she stepped out into the quiet hallway, she saw that the door to Jason's room stood open. Could he have just returned?

She went to peek inside. A maid in a stiffly starched green and white uniform was in the process of stripping the bed. Hearing someone in the doorway, she looked up.

"Good morning." Leigh smiled while her eyes searched the impersonal interior for a trace of Jason's occupancy.

"The man who has this room—has he gone out?" Leigh asked, hoping the maid might have seen him.

"I don't know, miss. I was just told to make up the room." With a shrug, she returned to her task.

A feeling of dread gnawing at her, Leigh rushed downstairs in a fever of impatience.

She asked the bored desk clerk to page Jason Randall.

"I believe he's checked out, ma'am. Just a moment, please." The ruddy-faced man turned to scan the set of square cubicles that lined the wall behind him. Locating the one he sought, he fished inside to pull out a small folded piece of paper.

"Are you Mrs. Randall?" he asked after reading the print. His boredom was replaced by an undisguised interest.

People surely are strange, he was thinking. A married couple, apparently, booked into separate rooms. And then, the man had taken off early today in a devil of a temper. Now here was the wife he had left behind, her face as white as paper.

"Are you all right, ma'am?" He saw her sway slightly and grip the counter for support.

She gave him a vague nod and reached for the note. The lounge area of the lobby was deserted at this hour of the morning, and not really caring where she sat as long as it was private, Leigh dropped down onto the first chair she came to and opened the piece of white hotel stationery.

"Leigh," she read, "I have to leave. Emergency. I'll send a car for you this afternoon."

Short and to the point, with Jason's signature scrawled in black ink across the bottom.

An emergency. Was it really an emergency? If so, couldn't he at least have wakened her and told her? A few seconds' phone call, that's all it would have taken. Wasn't it more likely that he welcomed a chance to get away from her, that he didn't want to face her again, she wondered with uncharacteristic cynicism. Was she now so repugnant to him that he couldn't stand a few hours' drive in her company? The words of

Paula Knight came unbidden into her mind, something about when Jason was through with a relationship, he was through. No recall. No recourse.

Well, she got the message. He had meant what he said last night. It was over.

Feeling numb, Leigh got to her feet and went back to the desk.

"Is there transportation from here to Harrellsville?"

"Yes, Mrs. Randall. A bus leaves twice a day from the village below the hotel." The clerk checked the large, round clock on the wall behind the reception counter. "You've got plenty of time to make the second run this afternoon," he said.

He told her the time and place and agreed to arrange for a hotel car to drive her the three miles to the village.

Leigh wasn't going to wait around to be picked up like an unwanted package someone had forgotten to claim. She'd make her own way back to Jason's house, and from there to New York. The way she felt right now, she wasn't going to stick around any longer than she had to.

After she had finished the rest of her packing, she called Smitty.

"Leigh!" Smitty registered surprise.

They exchanged the usual greetings and Leigh asked about Jody.

"She's fine. That picnic with the Penders did the trick. But what about you? Are you having a good weekend?"

"Smitty, is Jason there?"

"Jason? What would he be doing here? Isn't he with you?" Alarm sharpened her voice. "What's wrong?"

"Nothing much. Jason had to leave. Something came up. I'll explain when I see you." Leigh's hand was perspiring and slippery and she had to transfer the receiver to her other one.

"If Jason shows up there, would you tell him not to bother to send a car for me. I'll manage."

She had to break into Smitty's barrage of questions. "I have to go now. I should be there sometime this afternoon, Smitty."

Without hanging up the receiver, she pressed the button and dialed the desk to ask that someone be sent up for her bags.

The trip to Harrellsville seemed endless as well as exhausting to Leigh. It wasn't that she was really physically tired, although she hadn't had much sleep the night before, but her nerves were frayed. By the time the rather ancient, creaking bus pulled into the terminal in Harrellsville, all she wanted to do was to get away and forget that anyone named Jason Randall had ever existed.

She found a taxi to take her to the house, and by the time she finally arrived, the sun was setting in a blaze of color.

Smitty met her at the door, tall and gaunt, and totally dear to Leigh. At the sight of her uncompromising form, some of the remoteness that had allowed Leigh to keep going all day seemed to vanish and Leigh wanted nothing more than to put her head on Smitty's bony shoulder and have a good cry.

But of course she did nothing of the kind.

Smitty's sharp greeting put some starch into her instead.

"'Bout time you got here." The housekeeper said, reaching for Leigh's suitcase. She put it on the bottom stair and motioned Leigh into the kitchen.

"Now," she said, her hands on her hips, "I want to know what the dickens is going on."

Leigh sat down and gripped her hands tightly together in her lap. "I told you. There was some sort of emergency and Jason had to get back."

Smitty snorted. "I know that much. Jason was here about an hour ago. Dropped off his suitcase and had a sandwich. I guess he hadn't eaten all day. He said some workers had congregated at one of his warehouses early this morning, threatening mischief, so his secretary contacted him at Blackstones and told him he'd better come back. Apparently he talked some sense into the young fools."

"Where is he now?"

"That Paula was with him. He took her back to the office."

"Did you, er, give him my message?"

"About not sending the car for you? Yes."

"Did he say anything?"

"Just nodded and left." Smitty leaned her arms on the table, watching Leigh closely. "He was in a black mood. Should be, if you ask me. The very idea, going off and leaving you like that. You didn't ask to stay on there, did you?"

"No, I wasn't consulted."

"What's the man thinking of?" Smitty muttered. "What's the matter between you two?"

"Everything, Smitty."

The simple word hung on the air. *Everything.*

Leigh took a deep breath. There was a time to cut your losses, she told herself, and that time had come.

Taut with resolution, she asked Smitty, "Where's Jody?"

"At the Penders. Betty came for her after lunch to spend the afternoon."

"When are Bob and Clare supposed to get here?"

"Should be in the next few days. I expect they'll cable when they've got a flight."

"Do you think you could handle Jody as well as your work here until then?"

"If I had to." Smitty tensed with suspicion. "Just what are you planning, Leigh?"

Leigh couldn't meet her eyes. "Since Jody's parents will be here soon, then I've finished what I was asked to do." As she rose from the chair, she tried to smile, to hide the pain in her heart.

"I think I'll go upstairs and wash off some of the grime of the trip."

Smitty let her get to the swinging door before she spoke. "You're making a mistake."

Leigh swallowed hard. "Well, it won't be the first time, will it?"

Her decision made, she felt calmer. The tears that had threatened all day didn't come. Maybe I've just reached the bottom of my emotional barrel, she told herself as she turned the shower on full blast, as if she could wash Jason Randall out of her mind with the stinging spray.

She put on the white toweling robe that was hanging on the back of the bathroom door and hefted the suitcase she had brought from down-stairs up onto the bed.

No sense in unpacking it, but maybe she could fit in a few more items. She was leaving here with more than she had brought, literally as well as figuratively.

She had started on the second bag when the door opened.

"Just what do you think you're doing?" came Jason's harsh voice.

After a slight start at the sight of him, Leigh continued to fold a flower-patterned scarf.

"What does it look like I'm doing?" she countered coolly as she placed the small square of silk in the bag.

A glance at Jason showed her that he had moved inside the room, standing stiff and straight.

"So you're running away again?"

"No," she said, going over to the bureau near the window and opening a drawer. "I'm doing exactly what you yourself told me to do. I'm getting out of your sight."

With that, she made herself ignore his sudden indrawn breath and dipped into the drawer for a stack of blouses and tops. She didn't realize that he had come up behind her until he spoke.

"Don't go," he said.

"Wh—what?" Leigh whirled around, the pile of tops falling to the floor unheeded.

"Don't leave me." His dark eyes were burning into hers, pleading, and she had to station herself against the bureau to remain upright.

"If you leave, I don't think I can make it without you. You'd walk away from half a man,

183

because you'd be taking my heart with you. I love you, Leigh."

Half afraid she was dreaming, she went to him and put her hands on each side of his face, trying to read the message in his eyes.

"Jason," she whispered, going into his arms with a glad cry, as all the pent up hunger between them was released in a flood of passion. He held her as if he would never let her go, raining kisses on her eyelids and cheeks before his mouth claimed hers with an ardor that possessed and promised.

Too soon he held her away from him to look soberly down on her. "I owe you an apology for all the brutal things I said to you last night. I was crazy with jealousy. I wanted to strangle Morgan and the only way I could keep my hands off you was to get you out of there. I thought you were going to leave me and I didn't want to hear you say it. Then this blasted business at the warehouse came up and I knew I'd never be able to concentrate with you around, so I left you at the hotel, figuring we could straighten everything out later." Tenderly he brushed the soft clinging silver hair away from her face. "I know I hurt you and I'm sorry. I never want to hurt you again, Leigh."

"Jason, about last night . . ." she began, but he silenced her with a finger on her lips. "I know, Leigh. You had nothing to do with Morgan showing up at the hotel. I had a little talk with Paula. That's why I went back to the office this afternoon." His face was suddenly stern. "Paula's in the market for a new job."

"Oh, Jason, you didn't fire her for that!"

He shrugged. "Why not? Seeing Morgan in your room took ten years off my life. Besides, Paula seemed to have a few mistaken ideas about me and she was getting to be a pest."

Leigh laughed shakily. "You have no cause to be jealous of Dan or any other man, Jason. I love you. I think I always have."

"You do!" he cried exultantly, enveloping her in a swift hug. "Then why didn't you say so?"

The smile she gave him was dazzling. "Because I didn't think you cared."

He groaned. "Not care! God knows, I tried not to. How I tried! The trouble was, ever since I saw you at your grandfather's funeral I haven't had a moment's peace. My dreams kept being invaded by a tempting blonde. I would find myself thinking about you at odd times of the day and night. That's never happened to me before. I cursed myself for being all kinds of a fool, but it didn't matter. I still wanted you."

Leigh cuddled up to him. "You certainly hid it well," she teased.

He pulled her over to sit on the bed, keeping her close in the circle of his arms.

"I was scared," he admitted. "I didn't want to let myself in for what my father had suffered, putting my happiness in the hands of a beautiful woman." When he paused, Leigh nodded to let him know she understood about his father. Her fingers went up to tenderly cup his cheek.

"You were right, you know," he said slowly. "I didn't love you when I married you. Oh, the germ of attraction was there, but I was looking for a docile wife, one who wouldn't make demands. When you ran away, I was furious, but decided I was better off without you. Then I saw you again and got knocked for a loop." His eyes dwelt lovingly on her radiant features. "Your wanting an annulment gave me the perfect excuse. When I forced you to come here to take care of Jody, I intended to get you out of my system once and for all. Instead, you wangled into my heart. The way you cared for Jody, taking an interest in that old cottage." Wryly he shook his head. "You are some woman, Leigh. I was hooked but I didn't know how much until Dan Morgan appeared and tried to talk you into going back to New York with him. When I thought I might lose you, I realized how much I love you." She trembled in his arms.

"I had to make you stay—I couldn't wait for you to fall in love with me. But you had to stay willingly, because once I took you, I'd never let you go."

"My darling," she breathed, kissing him lightly, "this is too wonderful to be true."

"Believe it. It's true all right." Fiercely he pulled her to him. "As soon as Bob and Clare have taken Jody, we'll go away—to an island somewhere. It's time we started our life together," he said huskily.

Pressed so close to him she could feel his heartbeats, Leigh couldn't have agreed more.

Silhouette **Romance**

15-Day Free Trial Offer
6 Silhouette Romances

6 Silhouette Romances, free for 15 days! We'll send you 6 new Silhouette Romances to keep for 15 days, absolutely free! If you decide not to keep them, send them back to us. You pay nothing.

Free Home Delivery. But if you enjoy them as much as we think you will, keep them by paying the invoice enclosed with your free trial shipment. We'll pay all shipping and handling charges. You get the convenience of Home Delivery and we pay the postage and handling charge each month.

Don't miss a copy. The Silhouette Book Club is the way to make sure you'll be able to receive every new romance we publish before they're sold out. There is no minimum number of books to buy and you can cancel at any time.

Silhouette Romance

IT'S YOUR OWN SPECIAL TIME

*Contemporary romances for today's women.
Each month, six very special love stories will be yours
from SILHOUETTE. Look for them wherever books are sold
or order now from the coupon below.*

$1.50 each

Hampson	☐ 1	☐ 4	☐ 16	☐ 27	Browning	☐ 12 ☐ 38 ☐ 53 ☐ 73	
	☐ 28	☐ 40	☐ 52	☐ 64 ☐ 94		☐ 93	
Stanford	☐ 6	☐ 25	☐ 35	☐ 46	Michaels	☐ 15 ☐ 32 ☐ 61 ☐ 87	
	☐ 58	☐ 88			John	☐ 17 ☐ 34 ☐ 57 ☐ 85	
Hastings	☐ 13	☐ 26	☐ 44	☐ 67	Beckman	☐ 8 ☐ 37 ☐ 54 ☐ 72	
Vitek	☐ 33	☐ 47	☐ 66	☐ 84		☐ 96	

$1.50 each

☐ 5 Goforth	☐ 29 Wildman	☐ 56 Trent	☐ 79 Halldorson
☐ 7 Lewis	☐ 30 Dixon	☐ 59 Vernon	☐ 80 Stephens
☐ 9 Wilson	☐ 31 Halldorson	☐ 60 Hill	☐ 81 Roberts
☐ 10 Caine	☐ 36 McKay	☐ 62 Hallston	☐ 82 Dailey
☐ 11 Vernon	☐ 39 Sinclair	☐ 63 Brent	☐ 83 Halston
☐ 14 Oliver	☐ 41 Owen	☐ 69 St. George	☐ 86 Adams
☐ 19 Thornton	☐ 42 Powers	☐ 70 Afton Bonds	☐ 89 James
☐ 20 Fulford	☐ 43 Robb	☐ 71 Ripy	☐ 90 Major
☐ 21 Richards	☐ 45 Carroll	☐ 74 Trent	☐ 92 McKay
☐ 22 Stephens	☐ 48 Wildman	☐ 75 Carroll	☐ 95 Wisdom
☐ 23 Edwards	☐ 49 Wisdom	☐ 76 Hardy	☐ 97 Clay
☐ 24 Healy	☐ 50 Scott	☐ 77 Cork	☐ 98 St. George
	☐ 55 Ladame	☐ 78 Oliver	☐ 99 Camp

$1.75 each

☐ 100 Stanford	☐ 105 Eden	☐ 110 Trent	☐ 115 John
☐ 101 Hardy	☐ 106 Dailey	☐ 111 South	☐ 116 Lindley
☐ 102 Hastings	☐ 107 Bright	☐ 112 Stanford	☐ 117 Scott
☐ 103 Cork	☐ 108 Hampson	☐ 113 Browning	☐ 118 Dailey
☐ 104 Vitek	☐ 109 Vernon	☐ 114 Michaels	☐ 119 Hampson

Silhouette Desire
15-Day Trial Offer

A new romance series
that explores
contemporary relationships
in exciting detail

Four Silhouette Desire romances, free for 15 days!
We'll send you four new Silhouette Desire romances
to look over for 15 days, absolutely free! If you decide
not to keep the books, return them and owe nothing.

Four books a month, free home delivery. If you like
Silhouette Desire romances as much as we think you
will, keep them and return your payment with the
invoice. Then we will send you four new books every
month to preview, just as soon as they are published.
You pay only for the books you decide to keep, and
you never pay postage and handling.

Silhouette Romance

Coming next month from
Silhouette Romances

Strangers May Marry by Anne Hampson

Only Paul could help Laura keep her adopted child, but in return he demanded marriage! Was his price too high, or could Laura find true happiness married to a stranger?

Run From Heartache by Brenda Trent

Summer had lost her memory in the accident that brought Bracken into her life. But the past could never diminish her desire to share the future with this loving man.

One Man Forever by Juliet Ashby

Winging her way toward Paris with her new boss, Penny wondered if she could handle the job, and more importantly, could she handle the autocratic and devastating Pierce Reynolds?

Search For Love by Nora Roberts

He was suspicious, jealous, demanding and impossible! So why in heaven's name had Serenity lost her heart to her French cousin, Christophe, Count de Kergallen?

Island On The Hill by Dixie Browning

Frances had worked hard for her independence, and she wasn't about to give it up for a man. But rugged, handsome Cabel was more than a man—he was a lover!

Arranged Marriage by Brittany Young

Analisa had married Rafael Santiago out of respect for her dying father. But she hadn't anticipated the scorching flame of his love under the reddening Spanish sun.

READERS' COMMENTS ON
SILHOUETTE ROMANCES:

"I would like to congratulate you on the most wonderful books I've had the pleasure of reading. They are a tremendous joy to those of us who have yet to meet the man of our dreams. From reading your books I quite truly believe that he will someday appear before me like a prince!"

—L.L.*, Hollandale, MS

"Your books are great, wholesome fiction, always with an upbeat, happy ending. Thank you."

—M.D., Massena, NY

"My boyfriend always teases me about Silhouette Books. He asks me, how's my love life and naturally I say terrific, but I tell him that there is always room for a little more romance from Silhouette."

—F.N., Ontario, Canada

"I would like to sincerely express my gratitude to you and your staff for bringing the pleasure of your publications to my attention. Your books are well written, mature and very contemporary."

—D.D., Staten Island, NY

*names available on request